"Has it occurred to you that I might not find you attractive?"

"I retain this very vivid impression of how you felt in my arms—how you reacted," Sam replied. "And it wasn't repulsion, so don't fool yourself."

Ros bit her lip. "You caught me off guard, that's all."

"Excellent, because those defenses of yours are a big problem for anyone trying to get to know you—to become your friend."

"Which is naturally what you want." Her tone was sharply skeptical.

"Yes," he said. "But it's not all I want. Perhaps I want to discover everything there is to know—to explore you, heart, mind…and body."

SARA CRAVEN was born in south Devon, England, and grew up surrounded by books, in a house by the sea. After leaving grammar school she worked as a local journalist, covering everything from flower shows to murders. She started writing for Harlequin in 1975. Apart from writing, her passions include films, cooking, music and eating in good restaurants. She now lives in Somerset, England.

Sara Craven has appeared as a contestant on the British Channel Four game show *Fifteen to One*, and is also the latest (and last ever) winner of the 1997 Mastermind of Great Britain championship.

Sara Craven

MARRIAGE BY DECEPTION

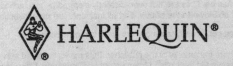

HARLEQUIN®

TORONTO • NEW YORK • LONDON
AMSTERDAM • PARIS • SYDNEY • HAMBURG
STOCKHOLM • ATHENS • TOKYO • MILAN • MADRID
PRAGUE • WARSAW • BUDAPEST • AUCKLAND

ISBN 0-373-12155-5

MARRIAGE BY DECEPTION

First North American Publication 2001.

Copyright © 2000 by Sara Craven.

CHAPTER ONE

SHE was late. Ten minutes late.

Sam checked his watch, frowned, and poured some more mineral water into his glass.

Perhaps she'd chickened out altogether. Well, he thought with a mental shrug, he couldn't entirely blame her. A list of the places he'd rather be tonight would run to several pages, plus footnotes.

He'd give her until eight-thirty, he decided abruptly, and if she hadn't shown by then, he'd go home. After all, there were plenty of others on his schedule—and she hadn't even been one of his choices for the short list either.

'Lonely in London', the ad in the *Daily Clarion*'s personal column had read. 'Is there a girl out there who's seriously interested in love and marriage? Could it be you?' And a box number.

As bait, it was well-nigh irresistible, and the replies had flooded in.

He didn't have a name for tonight's lady. Her letter had merely been signed 'Looking for Love'.

She'd been picked because she'd described herself as a beauty executive, and seemed younger than most of the others. And, he suspected, because her envelope bore a Chelsea postmark.

Which was why he was waiting here in the upmarket Marcellino's, rather than some more ordinary trattoria or wine bar.

He glanced restlessly towards the door out of the

restaurant, flinching inwardly as he caught a glimpse of himself in the mirror on the wall opposite. The cheap suit he was wearing was shining enthusiastically under the lights, his dark curling hair had been cut short and flattened on top with gel, so that it stuck out awkwardly at the sides, and gold-rimmed glasses adorned his nose.

I look, he thought, a total nerd—only not as good.

For a moment, the head waiter had hesitated over allowing him in. He'd seen it in the man's eyes. It was something that had never happened to him before, and he would make damned sure it never happened again when all this was over, he vowed grimly. When his life eventually returned to normality.

If it ever did, he amended, his mouth tightening. If he ever managed to escape from this mess of his own creation.

As for his intended companion for the evening—if and when she turned up, she would probably take one look at him and run out screaming.

He drank some more mineral water, repressing a grimace. What he really needed was a large Scotch, or some other form of Dutch courage. But the rules of engagement for tonight were strict. And he needed all his wits about him.

He looked at his watch again. Fifteen more minutes, he thought, and then I'm out of here. And they can't pass quickly enough.

Rosamund Craig sat tensely in the corner of her cab. They seemed to have moved about fifty yards in the past fifteen minutes, and now the traffic ahead was blocked solid yet again.

I should have set off earlier, she thought. Except

that I had no intention of coming at all. There was no need. All I had to do was pick up the phone and it would all have been sorted. End of story.

Now, here I am in a crawling cab with a galloping meter, going to meet a complete stranger. The whole thing is crazy. I'm crazy.

And the dress she was wearing was part of the madness, she thought, furtively adjusting the brief Lycra skirt. Usually she avoided black, and trendy styles. Taupe was good—and beige—and grey in classic lines. Discreet elegance had always been her trademark. Not clinging mini-dresses and scarlet jackets.

And these heels on her strappy sandals were ridiculous too. She'd probably end the evening with a sprained ankle.

Although that could be the least of her problems, she reminded herself without pleasure. And the most sensible thing she could do would be to tell the driver to turn the taxi round and take her back for another blameless evening at home.

She was just leaning forward to speak to him when the cab set off again, with a lurch that sent her sprawling back, her skirt up round her thighs.

Her particular die would seem to be cast, she thought, righting herself hurriedly and pushing her light brown bobbed hair back from her face. And it would soon all be over, anyway. She was going to have a meal in a good restaurant, and at the end of it she would make an excuse and leave, making it tactfully clear that there would be no repeat performance.

Honour on both sides would be satisfied, she told herself as she pushed open the gleaming glass doors and entered the foyer of Marcellino's.

A waiter came to meet her. '*Signora* has a reservation?'

'I'm meeting someone,' she told him. 'A Mr Alexander.'

She could have sworn his jaw dropped, but he recovered quickly, handing her jacket to some lesser soul and conducting her across the black marble floor to the bar.

It was busy and for a moment Ros hesitated as heads turned briefly to appraise her, wondering which of them was her date.

'The table in the corner, *signora*.' The waiter's voice sounded resigned.

Ros moved forward, aware of a chair being pushed back and a man's figure rising to its feet.

Tall, she registered immediately, and dark. But— oh, God—far from handsome. That haircut, she thought numbly. Not to mention that dreadful suit. And those glasses, too. Hell's teeth, what have I let myself in for?

She was strongly tempted to turn on her heel and walk away—except there was something about his stance—something wary, even defensive, as if he was prepared for that very reaction—that touched a sudden chord of sympathy inside her and kept her walking forward, squaring her shoulders and pinning on a smile.

'Good evening,' she said. 'You must be Sam Alexander—"Lonely in London".'

'And you're "Looking for Love"?' He whistled, his firm-lipped mouth relaxing into a faint smile. 'You amaze me.'

Slowly, he picked up the single red rose that lay on

the table beside him and handed it to her. 'My calling card.'

As she took the rose their fingers brushed, and she felt an odd frisson, as if she'd accidentally encountered some static electricity, and found to her own astonishment that she was blushing.

He indicated the chair opposite. 'Won't you sit down, Miss...?'

'Craig,' she said, after a momentary hesitation. 'Janie Craig.'

'Janie,' he repeated thoughtfully, and his smile deepened. 'This is a real pleasure.'

He might look like a geek but there was nothing wrong with his voice, she thought, surprised. It was cool and resonant, with a faint underlying drawl. And he had a surprisingly attractive smile too—charming, lazy and self-deprecating at the same time, and good teeth.

But his eyes, even masked by those goofy glasses, were the most amazing thing about him. They were a vivid blue-green colour—almost like turquoise.

I might have to revise my opinion, she thought. With contact lenses, a good barber and some decent clothes, he'd be very much more than presentable.

'May I get you a drink?' He pointed to his own glass. 'I'm on designer water at the moment, but all that could change.'

She hesitated. She needed to keep a clear head, but a spritzer wouldn't do that much harm. 'Dry white wine with soda, please.'

'A toast,' he said, when her drink arrived, and touched his glass to hers. 'To our better acquaintance.'

She murmured something in response, but it wasn't

in agreement. Sam Alexander wasn't at all what she'd expected, and she found this disturbing.

He said, 'You're not what I'd anticipated,' and she jumped. Was he some kind of mind-reader?

'Really?' she countered lightly. 'Is that a good thing or a bad?'

'All good,' he said promptly, that smile of his curling along her nerve-endings again. 'But I didn't have too many preconceptions to work on. You were fairly cagey about yourself in our brief correspondence.'

She played nervously with the stem of her glass. 'Actually, answering a personal ad is something of a novelty for me.'

'So what attracted you to mine?'

That wasn't fair, Ros thought, nearly spilling her drink. That was much too close to the jugular for this stage in the evening, and she wasn't prepared for it.

'It's not easy to say,' she hedged.

'Try,' he suggested.

She bit her lip. 'You—you sounded as if you wanted a genuine relationship—something long-term with real emotion. Not just…'

'Not just a one-night stand,' he supplied, as she hesitated. 'And you realised you wanted the same thing—commitment?'

'Yes,' she said. 'I—suppose so. Although I'm not sure I analysed it like that. It was more of an impulse.'

'Impulses can be dangerous things.' His mouth twisted slightly. 'I'll have to make sure you don't regret yours.'

He let the words hang in the air between them for a moment, then handed her a menu. 'And the next momentous decision is—what shall we have to eat?'

She felt as if she'd been let off some kind of hook,

Ros realised dizzily, diving behind the leather-bound menu as if it was her personal shield.

There was clearly more to Sam 'Lonely in London' Alexander than met the eye. Which was just as well, recalling her first impression.

However, sitting only a couple of feet away from him, she'd begun to notice a few anomalies. Under that badly made suit he was wearing a shirt that said 'Jermyn Street', and a silk tie. And that was a seriously expensive watch on his wrist, too.

In fact, instinct told her there were all kinds of things about him that didn't quite jell...

Perhaps he was an eccentric millionaire, looking for a latter-day Cinderella—or maybe she was letting her over-active imagination run away with her.

'The seafood's good here,' he commented. 'Do you like lobster?'

'I love it.' Ros's brows lifted slightly when she noted the price.

'Then we'll have it,' he said promptly. 'With a mixed salad and a bottle of Montrachet. And some smoked salmon with pasta to start, perhaps?'

Definitely a millionaire, Ros thought, masking her amusement as she murmured agreement. Well, she was quite prepared to play Cinderella—although she planned to be gone long before midnight.

The bar had been all smoked glass and towering plants, but the dining room was discreetly opulent, the tables with their gleaming white linen and shining silverware screened from each other by tall polished wooden panels which imposed an immediate intimacy on the diners.

At the end of the room was a tiny raised platform,

occupied tonight by a pretty red-haired girl playing popular classics on the harp.

As they were conducted to their table, Ros allowed herself a swift, sideways glance to complete her physical picture of her companion.

Broad-shouldered, she noted, lean-hipped, and long-legged. Attributes that disaster of a suit couldn't hide. He moved confidently, too, like a man at home in his surroundings and his situation. That early diffidence seemed to have dissipated.

She'd come here tonight with the sole intention of letting him down lightly, yet now she seemed to be the one on the defensive, and she didn't understand it.

As they were seated the waiter placed their drinks tenderly on the table, and laid the red rose beside Ros's setting with the merest flick of an eyebrow.

To her annoyance, she realised she was blushing again.

She rushed into speech to cover her embarrassment. 'This is lovely,' she said, looking round her. 'Do you come here often?' She paused, wrinkling her nose in dismay. 'God, I can't believe I just said that.'

'It's a fair question.' His grin was appreciative. 'And the answer is—only on special occasions.'

Ros raised her eyebrows, trying to ignore the glint in the turquoise eyes. 'I imagine you've had a great many of them lately.'

His look was quizzical. 'In what way?'

'Answers to your advertisement, of course.' She carefully examined a fleck on her nail. 'My—friend said you'd get sacks of mail.'

'There's been a fair response,' he said, after a pause. 'But not that many with the elements I'm looking for.'

'So,' she said. 'Why didn't I slip through the net?'

'Your letter intrigued me,' he said softly. He sat back in his chair. 'I've never actually met a "beauty executive" before. What exactly does it involve?'

Ros swallowed. 'I—demonstrate the latest products,' she said. 'And work on stands at beauty shows. And I do cosmetic promotions in stores—offering free make-overs. That kind of thing.'

'It sounds fascinating,' Sam said, after a pause. He reached across the table and took her hand. Startled, she felt the warmth of his breath as he bent his head and inhaled the fragrance on her skin. 'Is this the latest scent?'

'Not—not really.' Hurriedly, she snatched back her hand. 'This one's been out for a while. It's Organza by Givenchy.'

'It's lovely,' he told her quietly. 'And it suits you.' He paused. 'Tell me, do you find your work fulfilling?'

'Of course,' she said. 'Why else would I do it?'

'That's what I'm wondering.' His gaze rested thoughtfully on her face. 'I notice you don't wear a lot of make-up yourself. I was half expecting purple hair and layers of false eyelashes.'

'I look very different when I'm working. I hope you're not disappointed,' she added lightly.

'No,' he said slowly. 'On the contrary...'

There was a silence which lengthened—simmered between them. Ros felt it touch her, like a hand stroking her bare flesh. Enclosing her like a golden web. A dangerous web that needed to be snapped before she was entangled beyond recall. A possibility she recognised for the first time, and which scared her.

She said, rather too brightly, 'Now it's your turn. What do you do to earn a crust?'

He moved one of the knives in his place-setting.

'Nothing nearly as exotic as you,' he said. 'I work with accounts. For a multinational organisation.'

'Oh,' she said.

'You sound surprised.'

'I am.' And oddly disappointed too, she realised.

'Why is that?'

'Because you're not like my—any of the accountants I've ever known,' she corrected herself hastily.

'Perhaps I should take that as a compliment,' he murmured, the turquoise eyes studying her. 'Have you known many?'

The dark-suited high-flier from the city firm to whom she submitted her annual income and expenditure records, she thought. And, of course, Colin, with whom she'd been going out for the past two years. And about whom she didn't want to think too closely just now.

'A couple.' She shrugged. 'In my work, you meet a lot of people.'

'I'm sure you do.' He paused. 'But you've given me a whole new insight into accountancy and its needs. Maybe I should come to you for one of those make-overs.'

'Perhaps you should.' Involuntarily, she glanced at his hair. It was only a momentary thing, but he saw.

He said softly, lifting a hand to smooth the raw edges into submission, 'I did it for a bet.'

'I'm sorry.' Ros stiffened, flushing slightly. 'I didn't mean to be rude. It's really none of my business.'

'If that was true,' he said, 'you'd be at home now, microwaving yesterday's casserole. Instead of tasting this wonderful linguine,' he added as their first course arrived.

Yesterday's casserole would certainly have been the

safer option, she thought ruefully, as she picked up her fork.

'So, what I have to ask myself is—why are you here, Janie? What's the plan?'

She nearly choked on her first mouthful. 'I don't know what you mean. Like the others, I answered your ad…'

'That's precisely what I don't understand. Why someone like you—someone who's attractive and clearly intelligent—should feel she has to resort to a lonely hearts column. It doesn't make a lot of sense.'

'It does if you spend a lot of your time in isolation,' she said.

'But your working day involves you with the public. And men go into department stores all the time.'

A stupid slip, Ros thought, biting her lip. She would have to be more careful.

She shrugged. 'Yes, but generally they come to beauty counters to buy gifts for the women already in their lives,' she returned coolly. 'And when the store closes, like them, I go home.'

'You live alone?'

'No, with my sister—who has her own life.' She put down her fork. 'And I could ask you the same thing. You're employed by a big company, and a lot of people meet their future partners at work, so why "Lonely in London"?' She paused. 'Especially when you seem to have such low expectations of the result.'

'I'm sorry if I gave that impression.' He frowned slightly. 'Actually, I didn't know what to expect. You being a case in point,' he added with deliberation. 'Your letter was—misleading.'

Her heart skipped a beat. She tried a laugh. 'Because I don't have purple hair?'

'That's only part of it. On paper, you sounded confident—even slightly reckless. But in reality I'd say you were quite shy. So how does that equate with being a super saleswoman?'

'That's a persona I leave behind with the make-up,' she said. 'Anyway, selling a product is rather different to selling oneself.'

'You didn't think it was necessary tonight?' Sam forked up some linguine. 'After all, you claimed in your letter to be "Looking for Love", yet I don't get that impression at all. You appear very self-contained.'

Ros kept her eyes fixed on her plate. How did I think I would ever get away with this? she wondered.

She said, 'Perhaps I think it's a little early to throw caution to the winds.'

'So why take the risk in the first place?'

'Maybe I should ask you the same thing. You were the one who placed the ad.'

'I've been working abroad for a while,' he said. 'And when you come back you find the waters have closed over. Former friends have moved on. Your mates are in relationships, and three's very definitely a crowd. Girls you were seeing are married—or planning to be.' His mouth tightened. 'In fact, everything's—changed.'

Ah, Ros thought, with a sudden pang of sympathy. I get it. He's been jilted. So, I did the right thing by coming here tonight.

'I understand,' she said more gently. 'But do you still think a personal ad is the right route to take?'

'I can't answer that yet.' His smile was twisted. 'Let's say the results so far have been mixed.'

'I'm sorry.'

'Don't be.' The turquoise eyes met hers with total

directness, then descended without haste to her parted lips, and lower still to the curve of her breasts under the clinging black fabric. 'Because tonight makes up for a great deal.'

She felt her skin warm, her whole body bloom under his lingering regard. Felt her heart thud, as if in sudden recognition—but of what?

And she heard herself say, in a voice which seemed to belong to someone much younger and infinitely more vulnerable, 'You were right about the linguine. It's terrific.'

In fact, the whole meal was truly memorable, progressing in a leisurely way through the succulent lobster, the crisp salad and cool fragrant wine, to the subtle froth of zabaglione.

Ros was glad to abandon herself to wholehearted enjoyment of the food, with the conversation mainly, and thankfully, restricted to its appreciation.

Much safer than the overly personal turn it had taken earlier, she told herself uneasily.

She'd expected to find tonight's situation relatively simple to deal with. For a few hours she'd planned to be someone else. Only she hadn't put enough effort into learning her part. Because Sam Alexander didn't seem convinced by her performance. He was altogether far too perceptive for his own good—or hers.

And she was looking forward to the time, fast approaching now, when she could thank him nicely for her meal and leave, knowing she would never have to see him again.

And it had nothing to do with his awful hair, or the nerdy glasses, or his frankly contradictory taste in clothes. In fact, it was strange how little all those things, so unacceptable at first, had come to matter as the evening wore on.

And, in spite of them all, she still couldn't figure him for a man who would have to look too hard for a woman. Not when there was a note in his voice and a look in those extraordinary blue-green eyes that made her whole body shiver, half in dread, half in excitement.

But I don't want to be made to feel like that, she thought. Not by a complete stranger, anyway. Someone I'm not even sure I can trust...

'Would you like a brandy with your coffee?' Sam was asking. 'Or a liqueur, maybe?'

'Nothing, thanks.' Ros glanced at her watch. 'I really should be going home.'

'Already?' There was faint mockery in his tone as he checked the time for himself. 'Scared you're going to turn into a pumpkin?'

'No,' she said. 'But it's getting late, and we both have to work tomorrow.'

And, more importantly, something was warning her to get out while the going was good, she realised.

'You're quite right, of course,' he said slowly. His glance was speculative. 'Yet we both have so much more to learn about each other. You don't know my favourite colour. I haven't asked you about your favourite film. All that sort of stuff.'

'Yes,' she said. 'We seemed to skip that part.'

'We could always order some more coffee,' he suggested quietly. 'Fill in some of the gaps.'

She forced a smile. 'I don't think so. I really do have to run.'

'I'm sorry you feel that.' He was silent for a moment. Then, 'So, where are you based at the moment, Janie? Which store?'

She swallowed, as another pit opened unexpectedly in front of her. 'No—particular one,' she said huskily. 'I'm helping launch a new lipstick range—so I'm travelling round quite a bit.' She forced a smile. 'Variety being the spice of life.'

'That's what they say, of course.' He leaned back in his chair, his face in shadow away from the candlelight. His voice was quiet, almost reflective. It engaged her, locking her disturbingly into the unexpected intimacy of the exchange.

'But I'm not sure I agree,' he went on. 'I'd like to think that I could stop—running. Stop searching. That just one person—provided she was the right one—could give my life all the savour it needs.'

There was a tingling silence. Her throat seemed to close, and deep inside she was trembling, her whole body invaded by a languorous weakness. She wasn't used to this blatantly physical reaction, and she didn't like it. Didn't need it.

Let this be a lesson to me never to interfere again in other people's concerns, she thought, swallowing, as she called herself mentally to order. And now let me extricate myself from this entire situation with charming finality. And, hopefully, no hard feelings.

She gave a light laugh. 'Well, I hope you find her soon.' She pushed her chair back and rose, reaching for her bag. 'And thank you for a—a very pleasant evening.'

'I'm the one who's grateful. You've given me a lot to think about,' he returned courteously, as he got to his feet in turn. 'It's all been—most intriguing. Goodnight, Janie.'

'Goodbye.' She smiled determinedly, hoping he'd take the point. Politeness demanded that she offer her hand, too.

The clasp of his fingers round hers was firm and warm. Too firm, she realised, as she tried to release herself, and found instead that she was being drawn forward. And that he was bending towards her, his intention quite obvious.

She gasped, her body stiffening in immediate tension, and felt his mouth brush her parted lips, very slowly and very gently. Not threatening. Not even particularly demanding. Nothing that should cause that strange inner trembling again. But there it was, just the same, turning her limbs to water. Sending a ripple of yearning through her entire being. Just as if she'd never been kissed before. And as though she was being taught in one mind-numbing lesson where a kiss might lead.

When he raised his head, he was smiling faintly.

'No,' he said, half to himself. 'Not what I was expecting at all.'

She said between her teeth, 'Good. I'd hate to be predictable. Now, will you let me go, please?'

'Reluctantly.' His smile widened, but the turquoise gaze, boring into hers, was oddly serious. 'And certainly not without something to remember me by.'

He picked up the dark red rose from the table and tucked it into the square neckline of her dress, sliding the slender, thornless stem down between her breasts.

Then he stepped back, looking at the effect he had created. Seeing how the crimson of the flower gleamed against the cream of her flesh.

And a muscle moved beside his mouth. Swiftly. Uncontrollably.

She felt her nipples swell and harden against the hug of the dress, and had to bite hard on her lower lip to dam back the small, urgent sound rising in her throat.

He said softly, 'Janie—stay, please. You don't have to leave.'

There was the hot, salty taste of blood in her mouth.

She said huskily, 'Yes—yes, I do.' And barely recognised her own voice.

Then she turned and walked quickly away, across the restaurant and into the foyer. Knowing as she did so that he was still standing there, silent and motionless, watching her go. And praying that he would not follow her.

CHAPTER TWO

Ros let herself into her house. Moving like a sleep-walker, she went into the sitting room and collapsed on to the sofa, because, as she recognised, her legs no longer wished to support her.

'My God,' she said, in a half-whisper. 'What on earth did I think I was doing?'

Fortunately there'd been a cab just outside the restaurant, so she'd been able to make an immediate getaway.

Not that Sam Alexander had been anywhere in sight as she'd driven off, and she'd craned her neck until it ached to make certain.

But all the same she hadn't felt safe until her own front door had closed behind her.

And, if she was honest, not even then. Not even now.

I should never have started this, she thought broodingly. I should have left well alone.

Because men like Sam Alexander could seriously damage your health. If you let them.

And it was useless to pretend she hadn't been tempted. Just for a nano-second, perhaps, but no less potent for all that. Which had never been part of the plan.

Oh, God, the plan.

Unwillingly, her mind travelled back ten days, reminding her how it had all begun...

* * *

22

'Ros, just listen to this.'

As her stepsister hurtled into the room, waving a folded newspaper, Ros stifled a sigh and clicked 'Save' on the computer.

She said, 'Janie, I'm working. Can't it wait?'

'Surely you can spare me five minutes.' Janie operated the wounded look, accompanied by the pout, so familiar to her family. 'After all, my future happiness is at stake here.'

Ros eyed her. 'I thought all your happiness—past, present and future—was tied up in Martin.'

'How can I have a relationship with someone who won't commit?' Janie demanded dramatically, flinging herself into the chintz-covered armchair by the window.

'You've been seeing him for a month,' Ros pointed out. 'Isn't that a little soon for a proposal of marriage?'

'Not when it's the right thing. But he's just scared of involvement. So I've decided to stop being guided by my heart. It's too risky. I'm going to approach my next relationship scientifically.' She held up the newspaper. 'With this.'

Ros frowned. 'With the *Clarion*? I don't follow...'

'It's their "Personal Touch" column,' Janie said eagerly. 'A whole page of people looking for love—like me.'

Ros's heart sank like a stone. 'Including a number of sad individuals on the hunt for some very different things,' she said quietly. 'Janie, you cannot be serious.'

'Why not?' Janie demanded defiantly. 'Ros, I can't wait for ever. I don't want to go on living with our parents either. I want my own place—like you,' she added, sweeping her surroundings with an envious glance. 'Do you know how lucky you were, inheriting a house like this from Grandma Blake?'

'Yes,' Ros said quietly. 'But, given the choice, I'd rather have Gran alive, well, and pottering in the garden. We were—close.' She gave Janie a searching look. 'You're surely not planning to marry simply for a different roof over your head?'

'No, of course not.' Janie sounded shocked. 'I really need to be married, Ros. It's the crucial time for me. I wake up in the night, sometimes, and hear my biological clock ticking away.'

In spite of her concern, Ros's face split into a grin as she contemplated her twenty-two-year-old stepsister. The tousled Meg Ryan-style blonde hair, the enormous blue eyes, and the slender figure shown off by a micro-skirt and cropped sweater hardly belonged to someone on the brink of decay.

Sometimes she felt thirty years older than Janie, rather than three.

'Better your biological clock than a time bomb,' she said caustically.

'Well, listen to this.' Janie peered at the paper. '"High-flying, fun-loving executive, GSOH, seeks soulmate". He doesn't sound like a bomb.' She frowned. 'What's a "GSOH"?'

'A good sense of humour,' Ros said. 'And it usually means they haven't one. And "fun-loving" sounds as if he likes throwing bread rolls and slipping whoopee cushions on your chair.'

'Uh.' Janie pulled a face. 'How about this, then? "Lonely in London. Is there a girl out there who's seriously interested in love and marriage? Could it be you?"' Her face was suddenly dreamy. 'He sounds—sweet, don't you think?'

'You don't want to know what I think.' Ros shook her head despairingly. '"Lonely in London"? He's been watching too many re-runs of *Sleepless in Seattle*.'

'Well, you liked it.'

'As a film, but not to be confused with real life.' Ros paused. 'Janie—call Martin. Tell him you don't want to get married this week, this month or even next year. Let him make the running, and build on what you feel for each other. I'm sure things will work out.'

'I'd rather die,' Janie said dramatically. 'I refuse to be humiliated.'

'No, you'd rather run the gauntlet of a series of no-hopers,' Ros said bitterly. 'You could be getting into a real minefield.'

'Don't fuss so. I know how the system works,' Janie said impatiently. 'You don't give your address or tele-phone number in the preliminary contact, and you ar-range to meet in a public place where there are going to be plenty of other people around. Easy-peasy.' She nodded. 'But you could be right about the "fun-loving executive", so I'll go for "Lonely in London".'

'Janie, this is such a bad idea...'

'But lots of people meet through personal columns. That's what they're for. And I think it's an exciting idea—two complete strangers embarking on a voyage of mutual discovery. You're a romantic novelist. Doesn't it turn you on?'

'Not particularly,' Ros said grimly. 'On old maps they used to write "Here be Dragons" on uncharted waters.'

'Well, you're not putting me off.' Janie bounced to her feet again. 'I'm going to reply to this ad right now.

And I bet he gets inundated with letters. Every single woman in London will be writing to him.'

At the door, she paused. 'You know, the trouble with you, Ros, is that you've been seeing that bloody bore Colin for so long that you've become set in concrete—just like him. You should stop writing about romance and go out and find some. Get a life before it's too late.'

And she was gone, banging the door behind her.

Ros, caught in the slipstream of her departure, realised that she was sitting with her mouth open, and closed it quickly.

She rarely, if ever, had the last word with Janie, she thought ruefully, but that had been a blow below the belt.

She knew, of course, that Colin treated Janie with heavy tolerance, which her stepsister repaid with astonished contempt, but Janie had never attacked him openly before.

But then Colin doesn't approve of Janie staying here while Dad and Molly are away, she acknowledged, sighing.

He'd made it clear that their personal life had to be put on hold while she was in occupation.

'I wouldn't feel comfortable knowing that she was sleeping in the room opposite,' he'd said, frowning.

Ros had stared at him. 'Surely we don't make that much noise?'

Colin had flushed slightly. 'It's not that. She's young, and far too impressionable already. We should set her a good example.'

'I'm sure she knows the facts of life,' Ros had said drily. 'She could probably give us some pointers.'

But Colin had not budged. 'We've plenty of time

to think about ourselves,' he'd told her, dropping a kiss on her hair.

And that was how it had remained.

Suddenly restless, Ros got up from her desk and wandered across to the window, looking down at the tiny courtyard garden beneath, which was just beginning to peep into spring flower.

Her grandmother, Venetia Blake, had planted it all, making sure there were crocuses and narcissi to brighten the early months each year. She'd added the magnolia tree, too, and trained a passion flower along one wall. And in the summer there would be roses, and tubs of scented lavender.

Apart from pruning and weeding, there was little for Ros to do, but she enjoyed working there, and, although she was a practical girl, with no belief in ghosts, there were times when she felt that Venetia's presence was near, and was comforted by it.

She wasn't sure why she should need comfort. Her mother had been dead for five years when her father, David Craig, had met Molly, his second wife, herself a widow with a young daughter. Molly was attractive, cheerful and uncomplicated, and the transition had been remarkably painless. And Ros had never begrudged her father his new-found happiness. But inevitably she'd felt herself overshadowed by her new stepsister. Janie was both pretty and demanding, and, like most people who expect to be spoiled, she usually got her own way too.

For a moment Ros looked at her own reflection in the windowpanes, reviewing critically the smooth, light brown hair, and the hazel eyes set in a quiet pale-skinned face. The unremarkable sweater and skirt.

Beige hair, beige clothes, beige life, she thought with sudden impatience. Perhaps Janie was right.

Or perhaps she always felt vaguely unsettled when the younger girl was around.

Janie was only occupying Ros's spare bedroom because their parents were off celebrating David Craig's early retirement with a round-the-world trip of a lifetime.

'You will look after her, won't you, darling?' Molly Craig had begged anxiously. 'Stop her doing anything really silly?'

'I'll do my best,' Ros had promised, but she had an uneasy feeling that Molly would regard responding to lonely hearts ads as rather more silly.

But what could she do? She was a writer, for heaven's sake, not a nanny—or a minder. She needed her own space, and unbroken concentration for her work. Something Janie had never understood.

Ros had studied English at university, and had written her dissertation on aspects of popular fiction. As an exercise, she'd tried writing a romantic novel set at the time of the Norman Conquest, and, urged on by her tutor, had submitted the finished script to a literary agent. No one had been more surprised than herself when her book had sold to Mercury House and she'd found herself contracted to write two more, using her mother's name, Rosamund Blake.

Her original plans for a teaching career had been shelved, and she'd settled down with enormous relish to the life of a successful novelist. She realised with hindsight it was what she'd been born for, and that she'd never have been truly happy doing anything else.

With the exception of marrying and raising a family,

she hastily amended. But, unlike Janie, she was in no particular hurry.

And nor, it seemed, was Colin, although he talked about 'one day' quite a lot.

She'd met him two years ago at a neighbour's drinks party, which he'd followed up with an invitation to dinner.

He was tall and fair, with a handsome, rather ruddy face, and an air of dependability. He lived in a self-contained flat at his parents' house in Fulham, and worked for a large firm of accountants in the city, specialising in corporate taxation. In the summer he played cricket, and when winter came he switched to rugby, with the occasional game of squash.

He led, Ros thought, a very ordered life, and she had become part of that order. Which suited her very well, she told herself.

In any case, love was different for everyone. And she certainly didn't want to be like Janie—swinging deliriously between bliss and despondency with every new man. Nor did she want to emulate one of her heroines and be swept off her feet by a handsome rogue, even if he did have a secret heart of gold. Fiction was one thing and real life quite another, and she had no intention of getting them mixed up.

Life with Colin would be safe and secure, she knew. He'd give her few anxieties, certainly, because he didn't have the imagination for serious mischief...

She stopped dead, appalled at the disloyalty of the thought. Janie's doing, no doubt, she decided grimly.

But, whatever her stepsister thought, she was contented. And not just contented, but happy. Very happy indeed, she told the beige reflection with a fierce nod of her head. After all, she had a perfect house, a perfect garden, and a settled relationship. What else could she possibly need?

She wondered, as she returned to her desk, why she'd needed to be quite so vehement about it all...

Usually she found it easy to lose herself in her work, but for once concentration was proving difficult. Her mind was buzzing, going off at all kinds of tangents, and eventually she switched off her computer and went downstairs to make herself some coffee.

Her study was on the top floor of her tall, narrow house in a terrace just off the Kings Road. The bedrooms and bathroom were on the floor below, with the ground floor occupied by her sitting room and dining area. The kitchen and another bathroom were in the basement.

On the way down, she looked in on Janie, but the room was deserted and there were a number of screwed-up balls of writing paper littering the carpet.

Ros retrieved one and smoothed it out. '''Dear Lonely in London'',' she read, with a groan. '''I'm also alone, and waiting to meet the right person to make my life complete. Why don't we get together and—''' A violent dash, heavily scored into the paper, showed that Janie had run out of inspiration and patience at the same time.

Ros sighed as she continued on her way to the basement. She could only hope that 'Lonely in London' would indeed be swamped by replies, so that Janie's would go unnoticed.

In the kitchen she found the debris of Janie's own coffee-making, along with the remains of a hastily made sandwich and a note which read, 'Gone to Pam's'.

Ros's lips tightened as she started clearing up. Pam

was a former school buddy of Janie's, and equally volatile. No wise counsels would be prevailing there.

Well, I can't worry about it any more, she thought. My whole working day has been disrupted as it is.

Nor would she be able to work that evening, because she was going out to dinner with Colin. Which was something to look forward to, she reminded herself swiftly. So why did she suddenly feel so depressed?

'Darling, is something the matter? You've hardly eaten a thing.'

Ros started guiltily, and put down the fork she'd been using to push a piece of meat round her plate.

'I'm fine, really.' She smiled with an effort. 'Just not very hungry.'

'Well, I know it couldn't be the food,' said Colin. 'This must be the only place in London where you can still get decent, honest cooking at realistic prices.'

Ros stifled a sigh. Just for once, she mused, it might be nice to eat something wildly exotic at astronomical prices. But Colin didn't like foreign food, or seafood, to which he was allergic, or garlic. Especially not garlic.

Which was why they came to this restaurant each week and had steak, sauté potatoes, and a green salad without dressing. Not forgetting a bottle of house red.

'I hope you're not dieting,' he went on with mock severity. 'You know I like a girl to have a healthy appetite.'

Whenever he said that, Ros thought, wincing, she had a vision of herself with bulging thighs and cheeks stuffed like a hamster's.

'Colin,' she said suddenly. 'Do you think I'm dull?'

'What on earth are you talking about?' He put down his knife and fork and stared at her. 'I wouldn't be here if I thought that.'

'But if you saw me across a roomful of people would you come to me? Push them all aside to get to me because you couldn't stay away?'

'Well, naturally,' he said uncomfortably. 'You're my angel. My one and only. You know that.'

'Yes, of course.' Ros bit her lip. 'I'm sorry. I just have a lot on my mind at the moment.'

Colin snorted. 'Don't tell me. It's that girl causing problems again, I suppose?'

'She doesn't mean to,' Ros defended. 'She's just a bit thrown at the moment because she's split with Martin and—'

'Well, that's a lucky escape for Martin.' Colin gave a short laugh. 'And I hope a lesson for Janie. Maybe she won't rush headlong into her next relationship.'

'On the contrary,' Ros said, needled. 'She spent the entire afternoon replying to an ad in the *Clarion*'s personal column. "Lonely in London", he calls himself,' she added.

'She's mad,' Colin said. 'Out of her tree. And what are you thinking of to allow it?'

'She's over twenty-one,' Ros reminded him levelly. 'How can I stop her? And it doesn't have to be a disaster,' she went on, Colin's disapproval making her contrary for some reason. 'A lot of people must find happiness through those ads, or there wouldn't be so many of them.'

'Dear God, Ros, pull yourself together. This isn't one of your damned stupid books.'

His words died into a frozen silence. Ros put down her glass, aware that her hand was trembling.

She said quietly, 'So that's what you think of my work. I'd often wondered.'

'Well, it's hardly Booker Prize stuff, angel. You've said so yourself.'

'Yes,' she said. 'But that doesn't necessarily mean I want to hear it from anyone else.'

'Come on, Ros.' He looked like a small boy who'd been slapped—something she'd always found endearing in the past. 'It was just a slip of the tongue. I didn't really mean it. Janie makes me so irritated...'

'Oddly enough, she feels the same about you.' Ros leaned back in her chair, giving him a steady look.

'Indeed?' he said stiffly. 'I fail to see why.'

'Well don't worry about it,' she said. 'From now on I'll keep her vagaries strictly to myself.'

'But I want you to feel you can confide in me,' he protested. 'I'm there for you, Ros. You know that.' He swallowed. 'I'm booked to go with the lads on a rugby tour next week, but I'll cancel it if you want. If I can help with Janie.'

Ros smiled involuntarily. 'I appreciate the sacrifice, but it isn't necessary. I think the two of you are better apart. And the rugby tour will do you good.'

It will do us both good, was the secret, unbidden thought that came to her.

He looked faintly relieved, and handed her the dessert menu. 'I suppose you'll have your usual crème caramel?'

'No,' she said crisply. 'Tonight I'm having the Amaretto soufflé with clotted cream.'

He laughed indulgently. 'Living dangerously, darling?'

'Yes,' Ros said slowly. 'I think maybe I will. From now on.'

'Well, don't change too much.' He lowered his voice intimately. 'Because I happen to think you're perfect just as you are.'

'How strange,' she said. 'Because I bore myself rigid.'

She smiled angelically into his astonished eyes. 'I'd like brandy with my coffee tonight, please. And, Colin, make it a double.'

The days that followed were peaceful enough. Ros saw little of Janie, who was either working or at Pam's house, but nothing more had been said about 'Lonely in London', so she could only hope that the younger girl had thought again.

Colin departed on his rugby tour, still expressing his concern, and promising to phone her each evening.

'There's really no need,' she'd protested, a touch wearily. 'We're not joined at the hip.'

We're not even engaged, the small, annoying voice in her head had added.

'And I think we could both do with some space,' she'd gone on carefully. 'To help us get things into perspective.'

'Good riddance,' was Janie's comment when she heard he'd departed. 'So, while the cat's away, is the mouse going to play?'

'The mouse,' Ros said drily, 'is going to work. I'm behind schedule with the book.'

'You mean you're going to stay cooped up in that office all the time?' Janie was incredulous.

'It's my coop, and I like it,' Ros returned. 'But I am going out later—to get my hair cut.' She laughed at Janie's disgusted look. 'Face it, love. You're the party girl, and I'm the sobering influence.'

Janie gave her a long, slow stare. 'You mean if a genie came out of a bottle and granted you three wishes there's nothing about your life you'd change?' She shook her head. 'That's so sad. You should seize your opportunities—like me.'

'By replying to dodgy newspaper ads, no doubt,' Ros said acidly. 'Have you had a reply yet?'

'No,' Janie said cheerfully. 'But I will.' She glanced at her watch and gasped. 'Crumbs, I'm due in the West End in half an hour. I must fly.' And she was gone, in a waft of expensive perfume.

Ros turned back to her computer screen, but found she was thinking about Janie's three wishes rather than her story.

More disturbingly, she was questioning whether any of the wishes would relate to Colin.

A year ago I'd have had no doubts, she thought sombrely. And Colin is still practical, reliable and kind—all the things I liked when we met. And attractive too, she added, a mite defensively.

He hasn't changed, she thought. It's me. I feel as if there's nothing more about him to learn. That there are no surprises left. And I didn't even know I wanted to be surprised.

It was the same with the house, she realised, shocked. She hadn't needed to do a thing to it. It looked and felt exactly the same as it had when Venetia Blake was alive, apart from some redecoration. But that had been her choice, she reminded herself.

She found herself remembering what the will had said. 'To my beloved granddaughter, Rosamund, my house in Gilshaw Street, and its contents, in the hope that she will use them properly.'

I hope I've done so, she thought. I love the house, and the garden. So why do I feel so unsettled?

And why am I so thankful that Colin's miles away in the north of England?

I'm lucky to have this house, she told herself fiercely. And lucky to have Colin, too. He's a good man—a nice man. And I'm an ungrateful cow.

Janie bounced into the kitchen that evening, triumphantly waving a letter. 'It's "Lonely in London",' she said excitedly. 'He wants to meet me.'

'I didn't know you'd had any mail today.'

'Actually I used Pam's address,' Janie said airily. 'Covering my tracks until I've checked him out. Good idea, eh?'

'Wonderful,' Ros said with heavy irony. 'And here's an even better one—put that letter straight in the bin.'

Janie tossed her head. 'Nonsense. We're getting together at Marcellino's on Thursday evening and he's going to be carrying a red rose. Isn't that adorable?'

'If you like a man who thinks in clichés,' Ros returned coolly. She paused. 'What about Martin?'

Janie shrugged. 'He's called on my mobile a couple of times. He wants us to meet.'

'What did you say?'

'That I was getting my life in place and wanted no distraction.' Janie gave a cat-like smile. 'He was hanging round outside the store tonight, but I dodged him.'

'I just hope you know what you're doing.'

'I know exactly. Now all I have to do is write back to "Lonely in London" telling him I'll see him at eight—and pick out what to wear. I've decided to go on being "Looking for Love" until we've had our date.' She paused for breath, and took a long, surprised look at Ros. 'Hey—what have you done to your hair?'

'I said I was having it cut.' Ros touched it self-consciously. But it hadn't stopped at a trim. There'd been something about the way the stylist had said, 'Your usual, Miss Craig?' that had touched a nerve.

'No,' she'd said. 'I'd like something totally different.' And had emerged, dazed, two hours later, with her hair deftly layered and highlighted.

'It's really cool. I love it.' Janie whistled admiringly. 'There's hope for you yet, Ros.'

She vanished upstairs, and Ros began peeling the vegetables for dinner with a heavy frown.

This is all bad news, she thought. Janie may be using an alias, but Pam's address is real, and in an upmarket area. And I'm ready to bet that old 'Lonely' would prefer to target someone from the more exclusive parts of London.

This is not a game. It could have serious implications. But, apart from locking her in her room next Thursday, how can I stop her?

Janie threw herself headlong into the preparations for her blind date. She spent a lot of time at Pam's, coming back to Gilshaw Street only to deposit large boutique carrier bags. When she was at home she was having long, whispered telephone conversations, punctuated by giggles.

There was another communication from the wretched 'Lonely', which Janie read aloud in triumph over breakfast. It seemed her letter had jumped out from the rest, and convinced him they had a lot in common.

A likely story, thought Ros, sinking her teeth into a slice of toast as if it was his throat.

But when Thursday came Janie's shenanigans were not top of her list of priorities. She'd sent off the first few chapters of her book to her publisher, and had been asked to call at their offices to discuss 'a few points' with her editor.

She returned, stunned.

'Frankly, it lacks spark,' Vivien had told her. 'I want you to rethink the whole thing. I've got some detailed notes for you, and a report from a colleague as well. As you see, she thinks the relationship between the hero and heroine is too low-key—too humdrum, even domesticated. Whereas a Rosamund Blake should have adventure, glamour—total romance.' She had gestured broadly, almost sweeping a pile of paperbacks on to the floor.

'You mean it's—dull?' The word had almost choked Ros.

'Yes, but you can change that. Get rid of the sedate note that's crept in somehow.'

'Maybe because I'm sedate myself. Stuck in a rut of my own making,' Ros had said with sudden bitterness, and the other woman had looked at her meditatively.

'When's the last time you went on a date, Ros? And I don't mean with Colin. When's the last time you took a risk—created your own adventure in reality and not just on the page?'

Ros had forced a smile. 'You sound like my sister. And I doubt if I'd recognise an adventure even if it leapt out at me, waving a flag. But I'll look at the script again and let you have my thoughts.'

She let herself into the house and climbed the stairs to her study, carrying the despised manuscript.

Everything Vivien had said had crystallised her own uneasiness about the pattern of her life.

What the hell had happened to the eager graduate who'd thought the world was her oyster? she wondered despairingly. Has the beige part of me taken over completely?

The first thing she saw was the letter in Janie's impetuous scrawl, propped against her computer screen.

Darling Ros,

It's worked. I knew if I gave Martin the cold shoulder he'd soon come round, and he was waiting outside the house this morning to propose. I'm so HAPPY. We're getting married in September, and we're going down to Dorset so that I can meet his family. I'll E-mail the parents when I get back.

By the way, will you do me a big favour? Please call Marcellino's and tell 'Lonely in London' I won't be there. I've enclosed his last letter, giving his real name. You're a sweetie.

Love…

'''By the way'', indeed,' Ros muttered wrathfully. 'She has some nerve. Why can't she do her own dirty work?'

She supposed she should be rejoicing, but in truth she felt Janie had jumped out of the frying pan into the fire. She's too young to be marrying anyone, she thought.

Reluctantly, she unfolded the other sheet of paper and scanned the few lines it contained.

Dear Looking for Love,

I'm very much looking forward to meeting you, and seeing if my image of you fits. I wish you'd trust me with your given name, but perhaps it's best to wait.

'Perhaps' is right, Ros thought. Yet his handwriting was better than she'd anticipated. He used black ink, and broad strokes of the pen, giving a forceful, incisive impression. And he'd signed it 'Sam Alexander'.

She wished he hadn't. She'd had no sympathy for 'Lonely in London', but now he had an identity, and that altered things in some inscrutable way. Because suddenly real feelings, real emotions were involved.

And tonight a real man will be turning up with his red rose, she realised, only to be told by the head waiter that he's been dumped. And he'll have to walk out, perfectly aware that everyone knows what's happened. And that they're probably laughing at him.

Supposing he's genuine, she thought restlessly. He's advertised for sincerity and commitment, and wound up with Janie playing games instead. And maybe— just maybe—he deserves better.

She still wasn't sure when she made the conscious decision to go in Janie's place. But somehow she found herself in her stepsister's room, rooting through her wardrobe, until she found the little black dress and the shoes and thought, Why not?

There were all kinds of reasons 'why not'. And she was still arguing with herself when she walked down the steps and hailed the cab...

Now, sitting on her sofa, the black shoes kicked off, she castigated herself bitterly for her stupidity. She'd prophesied disaster—and it had almost happened. But to herself, not Janie.

She shook her head in disbelief. How could someone who looked like that—who dressed like that—possibly have got under her skin—and in so short a time, too?

Because sexual charisma had nothing to do with surface appearance—that was how.

And Sam Alexander was vibrantly, seductively male. In fact, he was lethal.

He also had good bone structure, and a fine body—lean, hard and muscular.

And she knew how it had felt, touching hers, for that brief and tantalising moment. Recalled the sensuous brush of his mouth on her lips.

For an instant she allowed herself to remember—to wonder... Before, shocked, she dragged herself back from the edge.

She shivered convulsively, wrapping her arms round her body, and felt the sudden pressure of the rose stem against her breast.

She tore it out of her dress and dropped it on the coffee table as if it was contaminated.

'You're not the adventurous type,' she said grimly. 'Back to the real world, Rosamund.'

On her way to the stairs she passed the answer-machine, winking furiously.

'Ros?' Colin's voice sounded querulous. 'Where on earth are you? Pick up the phone if you're there.'

For a second she hesitated then gently pressed the 'Delete' button.

And went on her way upstairs to bed.

CHAPTER THREE

SAM stood watching Janie's slim, black-clad figure retreat. He was aware of an overwhelming impulse to go after her—to say or do something that would stop her vanishing.

But you blew that when you kissed her, you bloody idiot, he told himself savagely as he resumed his seat, signalling to the waiter to bring more coffee.

He still couldn't understand why he'd done it. She wasn't even his type, for God's sake. And he'd broken a major rule, too.

But he'd wanted to do something to crack that cool, lady-like demeanour she'd been showing him all evening, he thought with exasperation, and find out what she was really like. Because he was damned sure the past two hours had told him nothing. That this particular encounter had bombed.

He'd had it too easy up to then, he thought broodingly. The others had been more than ready to tell him everything he wanted to know after just the gentlest of probing.

That was what loneliness did to you, he told himself without satisfaction. It made you vulnerable to even the most cursory interest.

But not Janie Craig, however. She'd simply returned the ball to his feet. And, unlike the others, she hadn't given the impression that the evening mattered. Less still that she hoped it would lead somewhere.

But perhaps there was something he could salvage

from the wreck. Something that would enable him to finish with this assignment and do some real work again.

If he was ever allowed to.

His mouth twisted bitterly. Six weeks ago he'd been lying in the back of a Jeep, covered in stinking blankets and protected by cartons of food and medical supplies, escaping from a Central African republic and the government troops who'd objected to his coverage of their civil war.

He'd come back to London, exhausted and sickened by what he'd had to see and report on, but secure in the knowledge of a job well done, knowing that his dispatches from Mzruba had made front-page news, under his photograph and by-line, day after day in the *Echo*. Expecting his due reward in the shape of the foreign news editorship that he'd been promised before he went.

His editor Alec Norton had taken one look at him and ordered him away on extended leave.

'Somewhere quiet, boy,' he'd rumbled, and tossed a card across the desk. 'This is a place that Mary and I use up in the Yorkshire Dales—the Rowcliffe Inn— soft beds, good food, and peace. I recommend it. Put yourself back together, and then we'll talk.'

Sam had gone up to Rowcliffe, a cluster of grey stone houses around a church, and walked and eaten and slept until the nightmares had begun to recede. The weather had been mixed—all four seasons in one day sometimes—but the cold, clean air had driven the stench of blood, disease and death out of his lungs.

He'd explored the two antique shops that Rowcliffe boasted, eaten home-made curd tart in the small tearooms, and visited the surprisingly up-to-date print works of the local paper, the *Rowcliffe Examiner*. He'd been beginning to wonder how he could ever tear himself away when a message had come for him from a friend on the *Echo* newsdesk via the hotel's fax. 'Houston, we have a problem.'

One telephone call later, his career had lain in ruins about him. Because Alex Norton was in hospital, recovering from a heart attack, and the *Echo* had a new editor—a woman called Cilla Godwin, whom Sam himself had once christened Godzilla.

She was far from unattractive. In her early forties, she had a cloud of mahogany-coloured hair, a full-lipped mouth, and a head-turning figure. Sam's nickname referred to her reputation as an arch-predator, cutting a swathe of destruction through one newspaper office after another, inflicting change where it wasn't needed, and getting rid of those who disagreed with her policies.

He'd no doubt she knew about her nickname, and who'd devised it. When it came to backstabbing, the newsroom at the *Echo* made the Borgias look like amateurs.

But he'd committed a far worse sin than that. During her stint as the *Echo*'s Features Editor she'd made a heavy pass at Sam, after an office party, and he'd turned her down. He'd tried to be gentle—to let her walk away with her pride intact—but she hadn't been fooled, and he'd seen her eyes turn hard and cold, like pebbles, and known he had an enemy.

And now she was the *Echo*'s boss, with the power to hire and fire.

He'd come back to London to find his foreign news job had been given to someone with half his experience, and that he was on 'temporary reassignment' to

Features, which was about the most humiliating demotion he could have envisaged. Cilla had told him herself, relishing every moment of it. She had never been magnanimous in victory.

It was virtual dismissal, of course. She planned to make his life such a misery that he'd be glad to resign. But Sam had no intention of playing her game. He had company shares, and belonged to the joint profit scheme, all of which he would forfeit if he simply walked out.

When he left, he meant to have another job to go to and a negotiated settlement with the *Echo*. Nothing less would do.

'Lonely in London' had been all her own idea, of course. It was to be, she'd told him, her eyes glinting with malice, 'an in-depth investigation of the women who replied to the personal columns'.

Sam had looked back blankly at her. 'It's hardly a new idea,' he'd objected.

'Then it's up to you to make it new,' she said sharply. 'We want real human interest material—tear-jerking stuff. You'll have to get close to them—explore their hopes, their dreams, even their fantasies.'

Sam shook his head. 'I don't think so. They've put themselves on the line already by replying. They won't want to discuss their reasons with a journalist.'

Cilla sighed. 'You don't get it, do you? As far as these women are concerned you're the real thing. A man searching for real love. You'll get them to trust you—and you'll get them to talk.'

Sam said quietly, 'You have to be joking.'

'On the contrary. Here we are with a new Millennium, thirty years of women's liberation, and yet they're still looking to find love with a complete stranger.'

'But I won't be a complete stranger—not if they're *Echo* readers,' Sam reminded her levelly. 'The name Sam Hunter and my picture were plastered all over the front page not so long ago.'

'I'm sure you're not that memorable.' Her smile glittered at him. 'But in case you're right we're going to use your middle name, so you'll be Sam Alexander instead, and we're going to alter your appearance too. Anyway, the women you meet will be eager—hopeful, not suspicious.'

'I think the whole thing stinks,' Sam said tersely.

Cilla regarded her manicured crimson nails. 'Are you refusing the assignment? I'd have thought it was ideally suited to your—peculiar talents.'

No, thought Sam, you know as well as I do that it's sleazy, and probably unethical, and you're waiting for me to say so. The trap's open and waiting. You want me to tell you to go to hell and walk out. Well, tough.

He shrugged. 'I can see problems.'

'There wouldn't be a story without them.' She leaned back in her chair, her gaze sweeping him. 'Just be certain none of them are of your making. It goes without saying that all these meetings take place in public.'

'Cilla,' Sam drawled, 'I wouldn't have it any other way. When do I start?'

He'd thought he was ahead on points—until he'd seen the clothes she'd chosen for him to wear—and the glasses—and also what the barber she'd summoned was doing to his hair.

'Sam isn't short for Samson, I hope,' she'd said gloatingly, as he was sheared. 'I wouldn't want you to lose your strength, darling. All that wonderful male potency I've heard so much about.'

He'd smiled at her in the mirror, his face aching with the effort. 'Keep listening, Cilla. I'll live to fight another day.'

Now, halfway through the assignment, he wasn't sure the battle was worth it. He was ashamed of what he was doing. He'd pick another civil war any day above those anxious, hopeful eyes looking at him across restaurant tables.

Maybe he should have cut his losses and gone, he brooded. Especially as instinct told him that 'Lonely in London' might be a picnic compared with other things Cilla Godwin could be cooking up for him.

He finished his coffee and asked for the bill. At least his expenses would give her a bad few minutes, but he needed to justify them by writing a really good piece on Janie Craig. And he wasn't sure that he could.

Back at his flat, he worked on his laptop for an hour, making notes about his meeting with her, but, as he'd feared, she remained totally elusive. He knew little more than she'd mentioned in her original letter—except that she blushed easily and wore a scent called Organza. And that her lips had trembled when he kissed them.

Not details he would put in his report, he decided sardonically.

Nor could he mention what had surprised him most about the evening—the moment when he'd asked her to stay—and found he meant it.

Sam snorted in self-derision, and switched off the computer.

The traumas of the past few weeks must have softened my brain, he thought, and went to bed.

*   *   *

Gardening, Ros thought crossly as she attacked the roots of a particularly hostile dandelion, was not having its usual therapeutic effect.

This should have been a really good day for her. After all, she would have the house to herself for the whole weekend, and the problem with Janie had been dealt with and could be put safely behind her.

She wasn't too optimistic about the future of this rushed engagement to Martin, but if it all ended in tears Molly and her father would be back by then, and could cope.

All in all, she should have been as happy as a lark. Instead, she felt thoroughly on edge—as if a storm was brewing somewhere.

The fact that she'd slept badly the previous night hadn't helped, of course. She'd been assailed by vague, tormenting dreams, none of which she'd been able to remember when sleep had finally deserted her altogether just after dawn.

Lying, staring into space held no appeal, so she'd done all the right, practical things. Made herself tea, showered and dressed in leggings and a big sweatshirt, eaten croissants with cherry jam, and started work.

Vivien had been quite right, she'd realised unhappily, as she'd put down the script a couple of hours later. A lot of the book seemed to have been written on auto-pilot. Yet the basic idea of two strangers thrown together in marriage for dynastic reasons was a strong one.

Normally she'd have revelled in every minute of it. Now she could see she'd just been going through the motions. The chemistry—the danger was lacking.

It was more than a question of a few alterations.

Her best bet would be to junk the whole thing and start again.

And she'd made a new beginning. In fact she'd made several. But when the only words she'd wanted to keep had been 'Chapter' and 'One', she'd decided to have a break and do some tidying in the garden.

She knew exactly what was to blame for this cranky restlessness. Last night's ill-judged rendezvous with Sam Alexander, that was what, she thought grimly. And let it be an everlasting lesson to her not to interfere.

Because he seemed to have taken up residence in a corner of her mind, and she couldn't shift him.

And the most disturbing thing of all was that she kept remembering him in ways that made her skin burn, and an odd trembling invade her limbs.

All things considered, she was quite glad she couldn't remember her dreams.

But nothing happened, she thought, irritably shovelling the defeated weeds into a plastic sack. We had dinner—and he kissed me. But that's no big deal. I should have seen it coming and dodged. My mistake. But there's no point in making a federal case out of it.

I'd be better off deciding what to say to Colin when he comes back tomorrow, she told herself, as she stripped off her gardening gloves.

Because she knew now, without doubt, that there was no longer any future in their relationship, and she would have to tell him so.

At first she thought she'd say it when he rang that evening. But that would be the coward's way out. The relationship might be irretrievably stale, but after two years he deserved an explanation face to face.

She wondered how upset he would really be. It had occurred to her some time ago that anyone who seriously wanted to marry Colin would have to get past his mother first. Colin's flat might be self-contained, but he was still where Mrs Hayton wanted him—on the other side of the wall—and she wouldn't let him go without a struggle.

The fact that this didn't bother me unduly should have warned me that things weren't right, Ros told herself. If Colin was really the man for me, I'd have fought for him tooth and nail.

She went indoors and made herself a sandwich lunch. She'd just sat down to eat it when the phone rang, making her jump uneasily. Just as she'd done with every other call that morning.

'Oh, pull yourself together,' she adjured herself impatiently. 'It can't possibly be Sam Alexander. You're being paranoid.'

'Ros?' It was Janie. 'I'll be back on Sunday night—probably quite late.'

'Everything's going well?'

'Ye-es.' Janie hesitated. 'Martin's parents are really nice, but I think I was a surprise to them. And they say it's too soon to be making wedding plans,' she added glumly.

'How does Martin feel?'

'Well, naturally he doesn't want to go against his family,' Janie said defensively. 'But we're trying to talk them round.' There was a pause, then she said in a lower voice, 'Did you contact "Lonely in London" for me?'

Ros swallowed. 'Yes,' she said. 'Yes, I did. I—I think he got the message.'

'You're a star,' Janie said. 'Must dash. We're taking the dogs for a walk.'

I don't feel like a star, Ros thought as she replaced the receiver. More like a black hole.

And why didn't I tell her the truth? I could have made a joke of it. Hey—I checked him out personally, and you had a lucky escape. A haircut from hell, and he buys his clothes from a street market.

She looked at her plate of sandwiches, decided she wasn't as hungry as she'd thought, and went back to her study.

But by mid-afternoon she still hadn't made any real progress on the rewrite of her book.

Maybe if I chose a different background, she thought. A different period—the Wars of the Roses, perhaps. Something that would give me a fresh perspective.

She'd need to do some research, of course, she realised with sudden relish, and a trip to the local library was infinitely more appealing than staring at a blank computer screen. Or allowing herself to become prey to any more ridiculous thoughts...

On her way down she grabbed her jacket and bag from her room, and went out, slamming the front door behind her.

As she went down her steps she looked in her bag, checking that her library card was there, so she only realised that someone was standing by her railings when she cannoned into him.

Startled, she looked up, her lips framing an apology, and stopped dead, gasping as she found herself staring at Sam Alexander.

'What are you doing here?' Her voice sounded husky—strained. 'How did you find me?'

'I went to the address on your last letter.'

'Oh,' she said numbly. 'Of course. And Pam's mother told you…'

'Eventually she did,' he said. 'Although she wasn't too pleased to hear her home had been used as a mail-box.'

'Why did you come here?' She was shaking, nerves stretched tautly. Shock, she told herself. And embarrassment, as she suddenly remembered what she was wearing—gardening gear and no make-up. She wailed inwardly. Because she was rattled, she went on the attack. 'And why aren't you at work anyway?'

'Why aren't you?' he countered.

Ros resisted an impulse to smooth her hair with her fingers. She didn't want to look good for him, for heaven's sake. 'I—I took a day off.'

'And so did I. So that I could find you. Because we didn't make any arrangement to see each other again.' He paused. 'In retrospect, that seemed a bad mistake.'

She lifted her chin. 'Then I'm afraid you've made another one, Mr Alexander.'

'Sam,' he told her quietly.

'Dinner was—nice,' she went on. 'But that's all there was. And it has to stay that way.'

'Why must it? You decided to reply to my ad.'

'A decision I now regret—bitterly.'

'I see,' he said slowly. He looked past her at the house. 'Are you married? Is that the problem?'

'Of course not.' Indignant colour flared in her cheeks.

'You were so cagey about your personal details, it seemed a possibility.' He gave her a meditative look. 'Living with someone, then?'

'I told you,' she said curtly. 'My sister. Now, will you go, please, and let us both get on with our lives?'

'But that's not how I want it,' he said softly. 'You see, I really need to find out about you, Janie. Last night was just a taste, and it made me hungry. And I'm convinced you feel the same, although you're trying to deny it.'

'Oh, spare me the psychobabble, please.' Ros drew a deep breath. 'Everyone's entitled to have second thoughts.'

'A word of advice, then. There's no point in describing yourself as "Looking for Love" if you run for cover each time someone shows an interest in you.' His face was solemn, but the turquoise eyes held a glint that the gold-rimmed glasses couldn't disguise. 'That contravenes the Trades Descriptions Act and involves a serious penalty.'

She'd assumed she was too tense to find anything remotely amusing in the situation, but she was wrong, she realised, as she bit back a swift, reluctant smile.

She said, 'Which is?'

'That you let me see you again.'

'You're seeing me now.'

'That's not what I mean.'

She said, 'Mr Alexander—has it ever occurred to you that it takes two to make a bargain—and that I might not find you attractive?'

'Yes, it's occurred to me,' he said. 'but I've dismissed it.'

'You,' she said, 'have an ego the size of the Millennium Dome.'

'And also a very good memory,' he returned pleasantly. 'I retain this very vivid impression of how you felt in my arms—how you reacted. And it wasn't re-pulsion, Janie, so don't fool yourself.'

She bit her lip. 'You took me off guard, that's all.'

'Excellent,' he said. 'Because those defences of yours are a big problem for anyone trying to get to know you—to become your friend.'

'Which is naturally what you want.' Her tone was sharply sceptical.

'Yes,' he said. 'But not all I want.'

'What more is there?' It was a dangerous question, but somehow she couldn't resist it.

'Perhaps—to discover everything there is to know.' His voice was soft, almost reflective. 'To explore you—heart, mind—and body.'

A shiver went through her, trembling along her senses, as if they were already naked together. As if his hands—his mouth—were touching her—possess-ing her. His body moving over hers in total mastery.

From somewhere she found the self-command to smile at him—a cool, even cynical curl of the mouth.

'A little over-ambitious for me, I'm afraid.'

'Fine.' His own grin was wickedly appreciative. 'Then I'll settle for meeting for a drink tonight in-stead.'

'Perhaps I already have a date this evening.'

'Then we'll fix it for some other time, when you're free. I can wait.'

'You don't give up, do you?'

'That,' he said, 'rather depends on my level of com-mitment.'

'And if I say—no?'

He shrugged. 'Then I'll just have to hang around here in the street, looking soulful and waiting for your heart to soften. The neighbours will love it,' he added, glancing round. 'We're attracting a fair measure of attention already. Curtains are twitching.'

She saw with annoyance that he was right. She said curtly, 'I could always take action against you for harassment.'

'But you were the one who contacted me in the first place,' he reminded her. 'And you came to meet me looking like a million dollars, as the head waiter at Marcellino's will confirm.'

'Which is more than can be said for you,' she countered waspishly.

But the jibe failed to needle him. Instead, he burst out laughing. 'What can I say? Anyway, no one would blame me for being smitten and trying again. I really don't think your harassment ploy would work—so why don't you give in gracefully?'

His voice deepened to a persuasive drawl. 'Come out with me, Janie, and I'll wear a wig—use contact lenses—start buying my clothes in Bond Street. See how desperate I am to reverse your bad impression of me?'

To her intense irritation she found she wanted to laugh too, and bit down hard on her lip.

She said, 'Mr Alexander...'

'Sam,' he corrected, quite gently. 'Say it for me—please?'

'Sam.' She heard the huskiness in her voice and took a deep, steadying breath. 'If we have this one drink, will you guarantee then to leave me alone?'

'No,' he said. 'But I promise I'll leave the ultimate decision in the matter entirely to you. And that I'll accept your ruling.'

'Very well,' she said. 'There's a wine bar a couple

of streets away called The Forlorn Hope. I'll see you there at eight.'

'Agreed.' His mouth twisted slightly. 'And I'll try not to read too much into your choice of venue. Until eight, then.'

'I'll be counting the moments,' she tossed after him acidly.

Sam swung back. Across the expanse of pavement, their glances met—clashed with the speed of fencing foils.

'No,' he said, quite softly. 'But one day—or night—very soon, you will. And there's another promise.'

She watched him go, aware that her breathing had quickened to danger level.

She thought, I want—I need him out of my life. Permanently. And tonight I must make certain that he goes.

CHAPTER FOUR

IT WAS only when he became aware that people in the Kings Road were giving him curious looks that Sam realised he was walking along wearing a broad grin.

'Get a grip,' he muttered to himself, as he hurriedly rearranged his features, and hailed a cab. You may have got a result, he thought, but it was too close for comfort. Which doesn't leave much to smile about.

More than once he'd lost the prepared script completely. Found himself saying something totally unexpected again. And by doing so he'd pushed the whole situation to the edge.

He'd need to tread more carefully that evening, he thought, removing the hated glasses and thrusting them into his pocket. He couldn't risk startling her into flight before he'd got all the material he needed for the feature.

His lips tightened as he recalled Cilla Godwin contemptuously flicking the piece he'd written back at him over her desk that morning.

'It's a cop-out, Hunter,' she'd declared. 'There's nothing of substance there. You haven't even touched on why she decided to go the lonely hearts route. There's more to this one than meets the eye, and you've missed it. See her again, and this time find out something useful.'

And Sam, reluctantly aware that her criticism was justified for once had gritted his teeth and nodded.

It hadn't really surprised him that tracing Janie

Craig had thrown up a complication. Perhaps all the others had used false addresses too, although he didn't think so.

No, he decided grudgingly, Cilla was right, damn her. Janie Craig was indeed something of an enigma— an irresistible challenge to any journalist.

And tonight, he realised, frowning, would probably be his last chance to solve the puzzle she presented.

He leaned back in his corner of the taxi and reviewed what he'd got so far.

Presumably she'd believed she'd covered her tracks sufficiently well, because she'd clearly been shocked to see him there, literally on her doorstep.

And what a doorstep, he reflected, his frown deepening. An elegant terrace house in a quiet cul de sac, which she shared with her sister. She could hardly support the upkeep of a property like that out of her freelance earnings, so the sister must be the one with the money.

Older? he speculated. Unattractive and sour about it? Jealous of her younger sibling, but reliant on her too? Not wanting her to find a man, perhaps, and make a life for herself, thus forcing Janie to subterfuge?

The possibilities were endless, but he had to establish the truth. And to do that he had to get Janie Craig to trust him. Something she'd not been prepared to do so far, he conceded ruefully.

And which he wouldn't manage by throwing down the gauntlet to her in the open street as he'd just done.

And, what was worse he'd no idea what had prompted him to challenge her in such an overtly sexual way. Any more than he knew why he'd kissed her at their first meeting—or begged her to stay...

And, not for the first time, he found himself wondering what the hell he'd have done if she'd agreed. And unable to produce a satisfactory answer.

One drink, Ros told herself nervously. That was all she was committed to, no matter what Mr Alexander's unbounded self-esteem might hope or believe.

And during the time it took to consume a single glass of wine she would make it abundantly clear that she never wanted to set eyes on him again, and that she would not hesitate to take legal action if he persisted.

And not even he could find her message ambivalent this time.

The whole sorry mess could so easily have been avoided if only—*if only*—she'd stayed quietly at home and minded her own business.

Instead she'd pranced off to meet him, dressed to the nines and sending out all kinds of misleading signals.

That black dress would be going to the nearly-new shop as soon as she'd had it cleaned, she decided grimly, and those shoes with it. She'd tell Janie there'd been some kind of accident, and reimburse her for them.

It was unnerving that Sam Alexander now knew where she lived. And she'd had to apologise abjectly to Pam's mother, who'd left a furious message on the answering machine, when she'd come back from the library.

And to think I complained that I was in a rut, she thought wearily. Welcome back dull normality.

Except that she didn't really mean it. And it was too late, anyway. Because her life had already changed quite incontrovertibly.

And, in some strange, confused way, she knew that even if she had the power to do it she would not change it back.

She was tempted to show up that evening in sweat-shirt and leggings again, but eventually swapped them for the conservative choice of a navy pleated skirt topped by a round-necked cream sweater. She looped a silk scarf in shades of crimson, gold and blue round her throat, and slid her feet into simple navy loafers.

She confined her make-up to moisturiser, mascara on her long lashes, and a touch of muted coral on her lips.

Neat and tidy, but definitely not seductive, she thought, taking a last critical look at herself.

She'd seriously considered following Janie's example, and packing a bag and disappearing for the weekend. But she guessed it would be pointless, and that in all probability she'd find him camped on her doorstep when she returned.

No, she would have to be brave and take her medicine.

She would be cool and firm, she told herself, as she set off on the short walk to the wine bar.

It was already crowded, and for a moment she thought he wasn't there, and felt her stomach lurch in what she instantly labelled relief. Because it felt dangerously like disappointment and that wasn't—couldn't be possible...

And then she heard a voice call 'Janie' above the hubbub of voices and laughter, and saw someone on his feet beside a table in the corner.

For a moment she thought she must have been mistaken, and misheard the name, because this man was a stranger.

Then she saw him smile, and realised it was indeed Sam Alexander.

But he's not wearing his glasses, she thought, as she threaded her way towards him through the busy room, her own mouth curving in reluctant response as she reached the table.

Little wonder she'd hardly recognised him, she thought, her brows lifting as she took in the unmistakably Italian cut of his charcoal pants, and the paler grey jacket he was wearing over a black rollneck sweater in what seemed to be cashmere.

She said a little breathlessly as she took her seat, 'You weren't kidding about Bond Street.'

'Their Oxfam branch,' he said promptly. 'Never let me down yet.'

Ros choked on a giggle. 'What happened to your glasses?'

'I left them at home. You made it clear I wouldn't have a menu to read, so I'm relying on you to decipher the wine list for me and stop me falling over the furniture.'

'It's a deal.' She shook her head. 'But you've let me down badly over the wig.'

'I looked like Mel Gibson in one, and George Clooney in the other. It didn't seem fair to expose you to that level of temptation.' He put up a hand and touched his hair. 'And this will grow out, I swear it.'

'But not,' she said, 'during the course of a solitary drink.'

'You never know,' he said. 'There could be a marked improvement by closing time.'

But by then I shall be long gone. She thought the words but did not say them aloud.

A waiter came hurrying up to the table, carrying an

ice bucket which contained, Ros saw, a bottle of Bollinger and two chilled flutes.

Sam said, 'I ordered in advance. I hope you don't mind.'

'Well—no,' Ros said slowly. 'But why champagne? This isn't exactly a celebration.'

He shrugged. 'You said one drink. I wanted it to be—special.'

'It's that all right.' She watched the waiter fill the flutes, and accepted the one she was handed. 'So what do we drink to?' she asked lightly. 'Ships that pass in the night?'

He said quietly, 'Let's start with—friendship.' And touched his glass to hers. 'Although we should really drink to you. You look—terrific.'

She gave a small, constrained laugh. 'That's because you're not wearing your glasses.'

'I can see well enough,' he said. The turquoise eyes travelled slowly over her. 'Terrific—and very different to last night—and this afternoon. How many women are you, Janie Craig?'

Embarrassed, she drank some champagne. It was cold and dry, and the bubbles seemed to burst in her mouth. Colin had never liked it, she found herself remembering. He complained it gave him indigestion. Something that seemed to belong to another lifetime— another age...

'I was going to write down a list of questions for you,' he said. 'So I wouldn't forget anything, or waste the short time we have together.'

'What sort of questions?'

'The kind that it usually takes days—weeks— months to answer. The basic things—do you prefer dogs to cats? Is spring your favourite season, or is it autumn? What music makes you cry? All the small details that make up the complete picture.' The turquoise met hers steadily. 'And that people find out about each other when they have all the time in the world.'

Ros forced a smile, her fingers playing nervously with the stem of her flute. 'And things that we don't need to know—under the circumstances.'

'So, let's cut to the chase instead.' He leaned forward. 'It's clear you're not seriously seeking a relationship, so why did you answer my ad—and why did you come to meet me?'

Ros hesitated, suddenly aware that she was strongly tempted to tell him the truth. But if she did, she argued inwardly, it would only lead to more and more complicated explanations, and recriminations—and what good could it possibly do anyway, when they were never going to see each other again?

On the other hand, she didn't want to lie either...

'Replying to the ad was someone else's idea,' she said, choosing her words with care. 'And once the meeting had been set up, I felt—obliged to go through with it.'

He said softly, 'So it was all down to your sense of duty.' There was an odd note in his voice which she couldn't quite interpret. It was almost like anger, but she didn't think it could be that, because he was smiling at her.

'But I suppose it serves me right for asking.' He paused. 'Are you seeing someone else?'

She hadn't expected that, and was jolted into candour. 'I was—but it's over.'

'And you used me to get rid of him—or was I simply to celebrate your new liberation?'

'Perhaps both—maybe neither,' she said. 'I wasn't thinking that clearly.' She hesitated. 'But I didn't mean to hurt your feelings. In fact that was the last thing I intended...'

'Well, don't worry about it.' His voice was silky. 'I expect I'll recover.' He refilled her glass. 'So, tell me about your sister.'

Ros jumped, spilling some of her wine on to the marble table-top. 'What do you want to know?' she asked defensively, mopping up with a paper napkin.

'She seems to have a fairly profound effect on you,' Sam said, his brows lifting as he watched. 'Is she your only living relative?'

Ros shook her head. 'My parents are abroad at the moment.'

'Ah,' he said. 'And you're house-sitting for them.'

'I'm taking care of things while they're away,' Ros agreed carefully.

Well, that explained the expensive house, thought Sam. It also meant she was still guarding her real address...

He said, amused, 'You're like one of those Russian dolls. Or an onion. Each time I think I've found you, there's another layer.'

Her mouth curved. 'I don't care for the comparison, but I think on the whole I prefer the doll. Onions make you cry.'

'Indeed they do,' he said. He gave her a thoughtful look. 'And I suspect, Miss Janie Craig, that you could break someone's heart quite easily.'

Ros studied the bubbles in her champagne. 'Now you're being absurd,' she said crisply.

'It always happens when I'm hungry.' He pointed to a blackboard advertising the dishes of the day. 'I'm having spaghetti carbonara. Are you going to join me?'

'We agreed—just a drink.' Ros remembered her abortive sandwich lunch, and her stomach clenched in longing.

'I'll let you slurp your spaghetti.' He shrugged. 'Or you can always go back to your lonely microwave. It's your choice.'

'Very well,' she said, adding stiffly, 'But I'm paying for my own meal.'

'That will keep me in my place,' he murmured, signalling to the waiter.

'And another thing,' Ros said, when their order, including herb bread and a bottle of Orvieto Classico, had been given. 'If you aren't wearing your glasses, how did you know that was spaghetti carbonara on the menu?'

Sam shrugged, cursing himself silently. 'In a place like this, it's practically standard,' he countered.

'Yes,' she said slowly. 'I suppose so.'

There were too many contradictions in this man, she thought, and they intrigued her. Or rather they intrigued the writer in her, she corrected herself hastily. And she could put the evening to good use by listening and observing.

'Have you always worn glasses?' she continued brightly.

'No,' he said. 'It happened very recently.'

'I suppose it's working with numbers all day.' Ros sighed. 'I expect using a computer is just as bad. I shall have to be careful.'

'You use a computer to sell beauty products?' Sam stared at her.

'Not exactly.' Ros gave an awkward laugh, aware

that she'd flushed guiltily. That was too much champagne on an empty stomach making her careless, she reproached herself. 'Just for—ordering—and sales reports. That kind of thing,' she improvised swiftly.

'Then I wouldn't worry too much,' he returned drily. 'I think your eyes will be safe for a long time yet.'

She gave a constrained smile, and stared down at her glass.

'But I can't say the same for your nervous system,' Sam went on. He reached across the table and took her hand lightly, his fingers exploring the delicate tracery of veins in her wrist.

'Your pulse is going like a trip-hammer,' he observed, frowningly. 'For someone who spends her life dealing with the public, you're incredibly tense. Are you like this with all the men you meet, or is it just me?'

All the men? she thought. Apart from a couple of totally casual relationships at university, there'd only been Colin...

She withdrew her hand from his grasp, clasping both of them tightly in her lap. 'I told you—I've never done anything like this before.'

'Then let's change the scenario,' he said. 'Let's pretend we did it the conventional way—that I saw you in a department store at one of your promotions, chatted you up, and arranged to meet you later. Would that make you feel more relaxed?'

'I—I don't know,' she said. 'Perhaps...'

'Then that's what happened.' His smile coaxed her. 'Forget everything else. This is just Sam and Janie, meeting for a drink and a meal, and examining the possibilities. No pressure.'

She lifted her head and looked at him, seeing how the laughter lines had deepened beside his firm mouth. She realised with sudden piercing clarity how much she wanted to touch them. How she longed to experience the entire warmth of his skin beneath her fingertips. To learn with slow intimacy the bone and muscle that made him. To know him with completion and delight.

And she felt dismay and exhilaration go to war inside her.

She said, breathlessly, 'Is that what you've said to all the others?'

The turquoise eyes looked directly into hers. His voice was quiet. 'What others?'

A silence seemed to enclose them—a small, precious bubble of quiet holding the moment safe.

A voice inside her whispered, Whatever happens—however long I live—whoever I spend my life with—I shall remember this.

And then the waiter came hurrying up with the platter of bread and the wine, and there was the fuss of cutlery and fresh glasses, and she was able to lean back in her chair and control her breathing, quieten the slam of her heart against her ribcage.

She thought, He said 'let's pretend'—and I will. I'll be Janie, and take the risk. Go where it leads—whatever the cost...

The Orvieto was clean and cold against her dry throat, and she swallowed it gratefully. 'That's so good.'

'Have you ever been to Italy?'

'Yes, I love it. I was there for nearly three months a year or so ago.' She halted abruptly, realising she'd given too much away again.

'Three months?' His brows lifted. 'None of the usual package tours for you, I see.'

'I was there to work,' she said. And it was true. She'd been researching her third novel, set at the time of the Renaissance and featuring an English mercenary who'd sold his sword to the Borgias until he lost his heart to the daughter of one of their enemies. Her trip had taken her all over the Romagna, and to Florence and Siena as well. The book had been fun to write, and had turned out well too, she thought, her lips curving slightly.

'Some of the big foreign cosmetics companies have—training courses for their products,' she added hastily, as she registered his questioning look.

'Do they now?' Sam drank some of his own wine. 'I didn't realise so much was involved.' He frowned slightly. 'You take your career very seriously.'

'Of course,' she said, and meant it. 'Don't you?'

'I certainly used to.' His eyes were meditative. 'But I seem to have reached some kind of crossroads. And I don't know for certain what my next move should be.' He added, 'I suppose you feel the same.'

'What makes you say that?'

He leaned forward. 'Isn't it why we're here together now?' he challenged. 'Because we know that everything's changed and there's no turning back?' He sounded almost angry.

She tried to smile. 'You make it sound—daunting.'

'That's because I'm not sure how I feel.' His voice was blunt. 'And, frankly, I'm not used to it.'

Ros bit her lip. 'Perhaps we should go back to Plan A—where you're "Lonely in London" again,' she suggested.

'No,' he said quietly. 'It's far too late for that, and we both know it.'

Her voice faltered slightly, 'You said—you promised—that you'd let me decide—and that you'd accept my choice.'

'Yes.' The turquoise eyes held a glint. 'Just don't expect me to take no for an answer, that's all.'

Bowls of creamy pasta were set in front of them, giant pepper mills wielded and dishes of grated parmesan offered.

She was glad of the respite, although nervousness had blunted the edge of her hunger by now.

I'm not a risk-taker by nature, she thought. How on earth am I going to get way with this?

'Eat.' Sam waved a fork at her when they'd been left alone again. His smile slanted. 'You need to build your strength up.'

'Please,' she said, her throat constricting. 'Don't say things like that.'

'Why not? Have you looked in the mirror lately? You have cheekbones like wings. A breath of wind would blow you away. And, oddly enough, I don't want that to happen.' He paused. 'As for the rest of it, you can call the shots, Janie. I won't push you into anything you don't want—or aren't ready for.'

'Another promise?' Her smile trembled as she picked up her fork.

'No,' he said, eyes and voice steady. 'A guarantee. Now eat.'

In the end, she finished every scrap of pasta, and followed it with a generous helping of tiramisu.

'That was wonderful,' she admitted, leaning back in her chair as their plates were removed.

'And the best part was when you finally stopped

checking where the door was,' Sam said drily, as he poured the last of the Orvieto into their glasses. 'For the first hour I was waiting for you to do a runner at any moment.'

She blushed. 'Was I that bad?'

'You were never bad,' he said. 'Just strung out.' He paused. 'How's the pulse-rate?'

'Calm, I think,' she said. 'And steady. At the moment.'

'Good,' he said. 'I'd hate to think I wouldn't merit a slight flutter—in the right circumstances.' He paused. 'Shall we have coffee?'

It was, she knew, a loaded question. The obvious response was, why don't I make some back at the house? And that, almost certainly, would be what he was waiting to hear. Hoping to hear. And yet...

The house was her domain—her little fortress. The place where she led her real life—not this pretence she'd been lured into.

To invite him back would be to breach some invisible barricade, and she wasn't sure she was ready for that.

It was all going too far, too fast, she thought, swallowing. One false step and she could be out of her depth—the waters closing over her head.

He said gently, 'Stop struggling, darling. The choice is between filter and cappuccino, nothing else. Though I wish...'

'Yes?' she prompted at his hesitation.

He shrugged. 'It doesn't matter.'

He'd been about to say, I wish you'd trust me, he realised ruefully, and he was in no position to ask any such thing.

It had been good to watch her start to relax—to

laugh and talk with him as if they were together for all the right reasons, he thought, as they drank their coffee.

Even so, he was aware that, mentally, she was still on guard. Emotionally, too, he told himself wryly. There was an inner kernel to this girl that was strictly a no-go area. That he suspected she'd fight to protect.

So, he would proceed with caution, and anticipate the eventual rewards of his forbearance.

There was silence between them, but it was a companionable silence, with neither of them believing they had to strive for the next remark.

He watched her covertly as she sat, quietly at ease, looking down at the green-gold of the strega in her glass. He'd told himself more than once over the past twenty-four hours that she wasn't his type, but now he found himself noticing with curious intensity that her mouth was soft, pink and strangely vulnerable now that she'd relaxed.

Her lashes, too, were a shadow against that amazing creamy skin. He imagined what it would be like to see all of it—to uncover her slowly, enjoying every silky inch—and found his body hardening in sharp response. Like some bloody adolescent, he mocked himself, dropping his table napkin discreetly into his lap.

But he had to be careful, because she still wasn't convinced about him, and he knew it. One wrong move and there was a real danger she'd blow him away. Which he didn't want, and, as he reluctantly had to acknowledge, not merely because he still had no clear understanding of her motivation or needs in replying to the personal ad.

While they'd been eating he'd tried to probe gently,

but had found himself blocked. She still wouldn't let him get too near. Or at least not yet...

And there had been a time when this would have suited him very well.

While he'd been a foreign correspondent he'd kept well out of emotional entanglements. He'd told himself it wasn't fair to keep a woman hanging around until he returned from yet another assignment, even if they were willing to do so—and, without conceit, he knew that there'd been several who'd been prepared to wait for as long as it took.

Only that hadn't been what he wanted—so he'd taken care to keep his relationships light, uncommitted and strictly physical, making it clear there was nothing more on offer. And inflicting, he hoped, no lasting damage along the way.

But this time it was different, although he had no logical reason for knowing it was so—just a gut reaction.

She glanced up suddenly and found his eyes fixed on her, and he saw the colour flare under her skin, and wondered if there was anything in his face to betray this swift, unlooked-for hunger that she'd aroused.

'More coffee, Janie?' He kept the words and the smile casual.

'No, thanks.' It irked her to hear him call her that, and had done all evening. In fact, she'd been debating with herself whether she should tell him her real name—indeed, whether she should come clean about the whole situation.

But the truth had no part in this game they were playing, she thought, with an odd desolation.

Besides, she wasn't sure how he'd react. He could be angry. Could even get up from the table and walk

out of the bar, and out of her life. Which would undoubtedly solve all kinds of problems. Except that she
wasn't ready for that.

'Then I'll get the bill and take you home.'

'I was going to pay half,' she remembered.

'We'll argue about that later.' He helped her into
her jacket, coolly, politely.

As the fresh air hit her, she felt suddenly giddy—
light-headed. Oops, she thought. I've had too much to
drink.

Two glasses of wine was usually her limit, yet tonight there'd been all that champagne before the
Orvieto had arrived. Had he done it deliberately? Was
this part of his grand seduction technique? She asked
herself as disappointment settled inside her like a
stone.

On the corner, she paused. 'There's really no need
for you to come any further. I'll be fine.'

His hand was firm under her elbow. 'I prefer to
make sure,' he said. 'One of my little foibles.'

When they reached the house, she found the bulb
had failed in her exterior light, and she fumbled trying
to get her latchkey in the lock.

'Allow me.' Sam took it from her hand and, to her
fury, fitted it first time.

'Thank you,' she said grittily.

'Don't say things you don't mean, Janie.' She could
hear the grin in his voice. 'You know you're damning
my eyes under your breath. Now, put the hall light on
while I check everything's all right.'

'Another of your little foibles, I suppose?' she
tossed after him.

'The age of chivalry isn't dead,' he returned, giving
the ground-floor rooms and basement area a swift in-

spection. At the door of the sitting room he paused, as if something on the other side of the room had engaged his attention. When he turned back to her there was a faint smile playing round his mouth, and dancing in his eyes. 'And to prove it,' he went on, 'I'm going to wish you a very good night, and go.'

She felt her lips part in shock. 'But...' she began, before she could stop herself.

'But you thought I was going to close the door and jump on you,' he supplied understandingly. 'And don't think I'm not tempted, but I noticed how carefully you were walking and talking on the way back, and I'd prefer to wait for an occasion when you know exactly what you're doing—and why—so that you can't plead unfair advantage afterwards.'

Ros walked to the front door and jerked it open. 'I'd like you to leave. Now. And don't come back,' she added for good measure.

He smiled outrageously down into her hostile eyes. 'You can't have been listening to me, Janie. I told you—I don't take no for an answer. Now, sleep well, dream of me, and I'll call you tomorrow.'

His hand touched her face, stroking featherlight down the angle of her cheek, then curving to caress the long line of her throat before coming to rest, warm and heavy, on her slender shoulder. It was the touch of a lover—deliberately and provocatively sensuous in a way a simple kiss on the lips would never have been. It was both a beckoning and a promise. A demand and an offering.

Ros felt the brush of his fingers burn deep in her bones. The ache of unfulfilled sexual need twisted slowly within her, and she knew that if he didn't take his hand from her shoulder she would reach up and draw him down to her. Take him into her arms, her bed and her body.

And then she was free, and freedom was a desolation.

She heard him say, 'Goodnight,' and the small sound in her throat which was all she could manage in response. And then he had gone, the door closing quietly behind him.

She leaned forward slowly, until her forehead was resting against the cool, painted woodwork.

She thought, What am I doing? What's happening to me?

And Rosamund Craig, the cool, the rational, could find no answer.

CHAPTER FIVE

Ros woke with a start, to find sunlight pouring through her bedroom curtains. She propped herself up on one elbow, pushing her hair back from her face and wondering what had woken her.

A peal on the doorbell, followed by some determined knocking, answered that.

'Who on earth can it be at this hour?' she asked herself crossly as she swung out of bed, reaching for her robe. Then she caught sight of the clock on her bedside table and yelped. It was almost mid-morning. And she'd known nothing about it. She'd still be deeply and dreamlessly asleep but for her morning caller.

'I'm coming,' she shouted, as she launched herself downstairs, kicking the morning mail out of the way and fumbling to unbolt her door.

She was confronted by a mass of colour. Red roses, she registered, stunned. And at least two dozen of them.

'Miss Craig?' The delivery girl wore a pink uniform, to match the small florist's van waiting at the kerb, and a professional smile. 'Enjoy your flowers. There's a message attached.'

Ros, her arms full of roses, shut the door and bent, with difficulty, to retrieve her letters from the mat. She carried the whole shooting match into her sitting room and curled up on the sofa, reaching for the tiny envelope attached to the Cellophane.

Sam's black handwriting filled the card. 'Your first rose looked lonely. I thought it needed friends, and we need each other. I'll pick you up for brunch at eleven on Sunday morning.'

Not so much an invitation as a command, Ros thought with exasperation. And what did he mean about her 'first rose' anyway? It had gone from the coffee table, so it must have been thrown away yesterday morning when the room was cleaned—mustn't it?

But she remembered the way Sam had paused in the doorway last night, and her gaze took the path his had done—straight across the room.

The rose, alive and well, in a narrow crystal vase, now occupied pride of place on her mantelpiece.

'Oh, God,' Ros said wearily. 'Manuela.'

Her Spanish cleaner was round, and smiling, and incurably romantic. To her, a red rose was something to be cherished, particularly if she suspected it came from an admirer.

And now Sam thinks that I kept it, she thought ruefully. Oh, *hell*.

She put the bouquet down on the coffee table while she opened her other post. As well as the usual junk mail there was a letter from her accountants, reminding her of the paperwork they'd need to complete her tax return, and a postcard from Sydney from Molly and her father, who were clearly having the time of their lives. She was still smiling as she opened the final envelope, which bore the logo of her publishers, and her smile widened into a grin of delight as she unfolded the sheet of headed paper and saw what Vivien had written.

As you know, each year *Life Today* magazine offers
a series of writing awards, and I heard yesterday
that *The Hired Sword* has been named the Popular
Novel of the Year. I'm so thrilled for you, Ros, and
you richly deserve it. I do hope you'll break your
rule about public appearances, and pick up the
award yourself at next month's ceremony.

'Try and stop me,' Ros said exultantly. Then
paused, as it occurred to her that the resultant publicity
would mean that her cover would be blown for ever,
and there could be no more Janie...

But there can't be anyway, she reminded herself
with a touch of grimness. Because the real Janie comes
back tomorrow night. And even if she didn't, all this
pretence still has to stop.

Last night had been—exciting, but also dangerous,
and she'd taken quite enough risks. Brunch was safe,
of course—a popular pastime for Sundays in the
city—and there would be no alcohol involved—but
when it was over she would tell him she couldn't see
him again. And she would produce some good and
cogent reason why this had to be—although she
couldn't think of one off-hand.

I've got all day, she thought, and frowned a little.
But why have I? Why am I not seeing Sam until tomorrow?

Which was not the kind of thing she should be
thinking at all, she reminded herself with emphasis.

She picked up the roses and carried them downstairs
to put them in water, then filled the coffee pot and set
it to percolate while she arranged them properly, her
fingers dealing gently with the long stems. They would
look good as a centrepiece for her dining table, she

told herself. They would not under any circumstances be going upstairs to her study—or her bedroom.

She put them on one side while she poured her coffee. She'd expected to wake with the hangover she deserved, yet in actuality she felt fine—as fit as a flea. And alive and—oddly expectant. As if something wonderful was going to happen.

But it already had happened, she reminded herself sternly. She'd won a prize for her Renaissance novel—a cheque and a silver rose bowl, if the award followed the pattern of previous years.

She didn't need anything else. Certainly nothing that might upset the even tenor of her days. She was a writer, and a successful one, and that was quite enough.

She carried her coffee upstairs, intending to shower and dress, but found instead she was continuing up to the top floor. She sat down at her desk and switched on the computer. The rewritten pages she'd been struggling with lay beside it, and she pushed them away, uncaring when they fell to the floor.

Her fingers moved to the keyboard—hesitated for a moment—then typed in: 'He had eyes the colour of turquoise'.

She looked at the words on the screen, and heard herself laugh out loud in joy and anticipation. Then she began to write.

It was only when the phone rang that she realised she'd been working for nearly two hours without a break.

Normally she'd have let the answering machine pick up the message, but she was sure she knew the identity of the caller, and she was smiling as she lifted the receiver. 'Hello?'

'Rosamund, is that you?' The aggrieved tones of Colin's mother sounded in her ear.

'Why, yes.' Ros was shocked at the depth of her own disappointment. 'How—how are you?' she went on over-brightly.

'Well, naturally I'm very upset, and so is my husband, but the physiotherapist has assured us there will be no lasting damage, so we can only hope.'

'Physiotherapist?' Ros echoed, bewildered. 'I don't follow.'

'You mean no one's told you that poor Colin's had an accident—sprained his ankle really badly? None of his so-called friends?' Mrs Hayton snorted. 'That rugby club. He should never have gone on that tour. Why didn't you use your influence—keep him at home?'

Because if I had done you'd have accused me of curbing his freedom, Ros returned silently.

She said, 'Did it happen in a match?'

'No, afterwards, during some stupid horseplay in the bar. The others were drunk, of course, and my poor boy bore the brunt of it. The physio saw he was hurt, and got him to hospital. Nobody else bothered. His ankle's been plastered to keep it steady, and now he has to rest it. He'll be on crutches for several weeks, I dare say.'

Ros was ashamed of the sense of relief flooding through her. With Colin laid up like this, it gave her the perfect opportunity to ease herself out of the relationship without any major confrontation.

'I'm so sorry,' she said guiltily. 'Please give him my—best wishes.'

'But you'll be coming round to see him, surely?' Mrs Hayton said sharply. 'We've turned our dining room into a temporary bedsit for him, because he can't manage the stairs to his own flat.'

'No, I suppose not. I—I'll try and get over tomorrow some time.' After brunch, she thought, piling up more guilt.

'I think he's expecting to see you this afternoon, Rosamund. I'm sure if the situation were reversed, nothing would keep him from your side.'

Ros groaned inwardly. 'This afternoon it is,' she said, glancing at her watch.

'But not too early,' Mrs Hayton cautioned. 'He's just had lunch, and I want him to have a good rest after it.' And she rang off.

On her way to Fulham, Ros decided that she wouldn't wait. That it would be fairer to tell Colin gently that this would be a good time for them both to stand back and consider their relationship.

She found him very sorry for himself. His thanks for the selection of paperback thrillers she'd brought him were perfunctory, and he was clearly more interested in his own woes.

'Nobody seemed to give a damn,' he declared petulantly. 'The physio looked after me—and brought me back here when I couldn't travel in the coach. I don't know what I'd have done otherwise.'

'How awful,' Ros murmured, wondering how to begin.

'The physio's been excellent,' Mrs Hayton said, coming in with a tray of tea. 'As soon as Colin's ankle has recovered sufficiently he'll be put on a proper exercise regime, with heat treatment.'

'Oh, good,' said Ros, noting with dismay that Mrs Hayton had settled down behind the tea and cakes.

Half an hour later, she was on her way home.

There'd simply been no opportunity for any private conversation. Colin's mother had stayed for the duration, confining the conversation to topics of her choice.

Did she think I was going to take advantage of him while he was helpless? Ros wondered crossly.

She'd tried to lighten the atmosphere by offering to autograph his plaster, only to be told by mother and son in unison that it was no laughing matter.

'I'm considering legal action,' Colin had added, frowning.

Ros had been glad to swallow her cup of weak tea, and the rather dry scone, and go.

Colin hadn't even asked when her next visit would be. He took it for granted that she would simply slot in on some rota of his mother's devising.

And a month ago—even ten days ago—she probably would have done so.

But now, suddenly, she wasn't the same person any longer. All the small dissatisfactions of her life had snowballed into this need for change. A need that had left Colin behind, yet promised nothing for the future.

But I'll always have my work, she rallied herself. And paused as she faced, for the first time, the possibility that it might no longer be enough.

'I don't know what to do,' Sam said.

Alex Norton, his former editor, on the road to recovery in a private clinic, peered at him over his glasses. 'Well, you can't stay on the *Echo*, that's for sure. So far, all Cilla's done is cut your hair. Next time she might go for complete emasculation.' And he chuckled.

'I wish I was dead.' Sam helped himself to some grapes from the bowl on the bedside trolley.

'No, you don't,' Alex corrected him robustly. 'Because I've been close, and I don't recommend it. But you won't rescue your career while Ms Godwin's in control. You made a bad enemy there, so you may as well cut your losses. Find another job and settle for the best severance deal you can get.' He paused. 'How did you like Rowcliffe?'

'I wish I'd never left it,' Sam said bleakly.

Alex nodded. 'I always felt the same. In fact, I had this dream that I'd wind up there, editing that weekly paper of theirs—the *Rowcliffe Examiner*.' He shook his head. 'Some hope, of course. You couldn't prise my Mary out of London, bless her. But it would have been a good life.' He shot Sam a look. 'Does it still exist—the *Examiner*?'

'Absolutely. It was required reading at the hotel,' Sam returned. 'And it still has the local farm prices and auctions on the front page.'

'Ah,' Alex leaned back against his pillows. 'I'm glad some things don't change. And, who knows? With a bit of luck you might find yourself back there—one of these days.'

'Not soon enough,' Sam said bitterly.

He was repeating these words under his breath as he let himself back into his flat that night. He'd had an appointment with one of the final names on his list. She'd provided plenty of good material, but the evening had ended in total disaster. He caught a glimpse of himself in the hall mirror and shuddered. At least he'd never be able to wear this ghastly suit again, so every cloud did have a silver lining.

He went into the bathroom, stripped and showered, letting the water cascade over him until he felt clean again. Then he put on his robe, made some coffee, and went into the living room to work on his laptop.

He'd just started when his door buzzer sounded. Startled, he glanced at his watch, wondering who could be calling so late. It was probably Mrs Ferguson, the elderly widow in the adjoining flat, wanting him to change a lightbulb, or adjust her trip-switch, or some other minor task. She was a sweet soul, and lonely, and it was a pleasure to keep an eye on her. But he wished she'd restrict her requests for help to sociable hours.

However, he was smiling when he opened the door. Until he saw who was standing outside.

'Good evening.' Cilla Godwin was smiling too, her eyes calculating as she looked him over. 'May I come in?'

He said levelly, 'If you wish,' and stood aside to give her access, resisting the impulse to tighten the belt of his robe. She walked ahead of him into the lamplit sitting room.

'Very stylish,' she said, looking round her. 'Do you share with anyone?'

'Not since my last flatmate got married,' he said. 'What can I do for you, Ms Godwin?'

'Don't be formal, Sam, you're not dressed for it.' She looked at the glass standing beside his laptop. 'If that's whiskey, I'll have one too.'

Sam found the bottle of Jameson's and splashed a measure into a cut-glass tumbler. 'Do I take it this is a social call?'

'Oh, I have various reasons for being here.' She accepted the glass from him. 'Cheers.'

'May I know what they are? As you can see, I am trying to work.'

'You were out interviewing tonight? Who was she?'

'A divorcee called Mandy, with a chip on her shoulder and a frank tongue.'

'Sounds ideal. Did it go well?'

'Until the last ten minutes, when she made it clear she expected the evening to end in bed,' Sam said pleasantly. 'When she found out it wasn't going to happen, she started throwing things—the remains of a carafe of red wine and half a pot of cold coffee for starters. We were lucky not to be arrested, and we certainly can't use Albertine's as a venue again. I've written you a memo.

'Oh, and the office suit is a write-off,' he added. 'So unless you want to ask the charity shop for another, I'll be wearing my own clothes from now on.'

'What is this strange power you have over women?' She was smiling again, and Sam's warning antennae were going into overdrive. 'Even when you look like a geek, they're queuing to get laid.'

'I wouldn't use Mandy as a criterion,' Sam said drily. 'I got the impression anyone would have done.'

'You're far too modest.' She took a seat on the sofa, crossing her legs. She was wearing a brief black skirt, topped by a matching camisole, and a white jacket like a man's tuxedo. She had swept her hair up into a loose knot, and her nails and mouth were painted a dark, challenging red.

War paint, thought Sam.

He kept his voice even. 'But then, according to you, I have so much to be modest about.' He retrieved his glass from the table and went to stand by the fireplace.

Not two swords' lengths apart, but the best he could manage.

She laughed. 'Poor Sam—does that still rankle? But I'm having to eat my words. I was notified today that you've been voted Journalist of the Year by *Life Today* magazine for your Mzruba work.' She paused. 'I told the proprietor, and he was well pleased. Asked what you were doing at the moment.' She shrugged. 'I said—a special assignment.'

'The perfect description.' Sam drank some whiskey.

'I thought so.' Cilla leaned back against the cushions, the drag of her camisole revealing that she was bra-less.

She was showing a fair amount of thigh as well, Sam realised bleakly. Surely lightning wasn't going to strike him twice.

'But if you're going to win awards, maybe I should be making better use of you.' Her tone was meditative, her smile cat-like. 'Sam—we don't have to be on bad terms—do we?'

He was instantly wary. 'Of course not.' He added a polite smile. 'It was good of you to come and tell me about the award, Cilla, but I mustn't keep you. It's Saturday night, after all, and I'm sure you have places to go and people to see.'

Like your husband, he added silently. He knew she had one—somewhere—but the basis for their relationship was anyone's guess.

'Mark's out of his depth on the foreign news desk,' she went on, as if he hadn't spoken. 'I'm going to move him, so there'll be a vacancy again. And this time I need to be sure that the right man gets the job.' Her voice deepened, became husky. 'Do you think you're that man, Sam? As we've had our differences in the past, I'd need to assure myself that you'd be—loyal.'

She invested that final word with a whole host of meanings.

Sam leaned a shoulder against the mantelshelf and stared at his whiskey. All he had to do was walk across and sit down beside her and that long-promised promotion would be his—but at a price. It would be a totally cynical encounter—an exercise in sexuality—and not the first to come his way, admittedly. Yet all he could feel was a profound distaste as cold and bitter as gall.

'I promise you the best foreign news coverage anywhere,' he said quietly. 'I hope that's enough, because it's all there is.'

There was a long silence. Her smile, when it came, would have eaten through metal. 'I think, Sam darling, that you've just made a terrible mistake.'

'No,' he said. 'I've just avoided a worse one.'

'Is this your night for turning women down? First the divorcee and now me.' Her hands moved in a brief angry gesture she could not control. The dark enamel on her fingertips looked, he thought, like dried blood.

'But perhaps you have a different agenda altogether,' she went on. 'Maybe you simply prefer other men.'

She was trying to make him angry, he thought. To provoke him into something hasty.

He shrugged. 'Or maybe I'm old-fashioned enough to want to do my own hunting. Have you ever thought of that, Ms Godwin?'

She got quickly and almost clumsily to her feet. 'I shall expect your resignation on my desk on Monday.'

'No,' he said. 'I'm not ready to do that. You'll have to fire me, and at the moment you have no grounds.'

At the door, she gave him a last venomous look. 'Enjoy your little bit of glory over the award,' she said. 'By the time I've finished with you, you'll be a standing joke.'

He said wearily, 'I'm sure you'll try. Goodnight, Cilla.'

It hurt to breathe, he discovered when he was alone, and he felt slightly nauseous.

I never saw that coming, he told himself grimly.

In fact, he could hardly believe it had happened. That it hadn't all been a ghastly hallucination.

Except for the evidence. Picking up the lipstick-stained glass she'd been using between his thumb and forefinger, he took it into the kitchen and dropped it into the wastebin.

Hell hath no fury like a woman scorned—as he'd already found out to his cost that evening. And in Cilla Godwin's case it had happened twice.

He wondered wryly what kind of hell he could expect. Certainly his days on the *Echo* were numbered, but he'd known that already. He'd start looking round for another job on Monday.

The heavy, musky scent she'd been wearing still seemed to hang in the sitting room, he realised, wrinkling his nose. He unlocked the window and opened it wide. The air that flooded it was cold but stale.

I haven't breathed properly since I came back from Rowcliffe, he thought restlessly, as he went back to his laptop.

He read what he'd written, then with an impatient exclamation deleted it all. He'd turned Mandy into a caricature, he thought. The man-hungry blonde. What he'd seen, but hadn't shown, was the pain of her divorce, and her fear of a lonely future.

He'd had compassion enough for the innocents caught up in the Mzruban civil war. Surely he could spare some for Mandy, suffering the after effects of a more personal conflict.

He stared at the empty screen, trying to recreate her image, but the girl's face that swam in his vision was a very different one—pale-skinned and hazel-eyed, with a smile that tugged at some inner heart-cord he hadn't known he possessed.

He swore under his breath. This was a complication he didn't need—particularly when his whole life was at a crossroads.

Janie Craig had started off as a puzzle he'd been determined to solve. But finding the real girl behind the façade had turned into a much more personal quest. Which had somehow been crystallised when he saw she'd kept the rose he'd given her.

But that didn't mean he'd had to surrender to his impulse to deluge her with flowers, he derided himself. She wasn't his type and that wasn't his style.

And it has to stop right here and now, he told himself grimly. Before it really starts running out of control.

Tomorrow would be the last time they saw each other, and he had decided exactly how he would handle it. Locked into her usual environment, she had no reason to lower her guard, he thought, as he switched off the computer. So he would try a different ploy to break down her defences.

A change of surroundings, he mused with satisfaction. A change of approach. Before they walked away from each other.

He hadn't forgotten that she'd told him she'd only kept their first appointment from a sense of obligation. It would be tempting to see if he could induce her to feel just an atom of regret when they parted from each other for ever.

But her smile continued to haunt him, even in sleep, and he woke with a start, realising that he had turned to her, reaching for her in yearning and need, only to encounter the chill emptiness in the bed beside him.

CHAPTER SIX

Ros glanced at the pile of discarded clothing on her bed and groaned.

Look in the mirror, she adjured herself sternly, and say after me—this is only a brunch. It is no big deal.

She'd tried on nearly everything she owned, and rejected it. Now she was back to her original choice, a pair of slim-fitting cream pants and a matching V-neck sweater. Cool and casual, she thought, hooking her favourite amber earrings into her lobes, to complement a day when the sky was almost cloudless and there was real warmth in the spring sun.

It was a long time since she'd been out to a brunch. Not, in fact, since her trip to New York to meet her American publishers, when she'd spent a gloriously relaxed Sunday morning in Greenwich Village.

She wondered if Sam's travels had ever taken him to the States.

There was so much about him she didn't know—and probably never would, she realised with a sudden pang. So she would simply have to invent it. And she had a head start on that already.

She had written until late the previous night, watching the story catch fire, feeling her excitement—her empathy with it—build swiftly and surely.

All it needed was a new hero, she thought, applying a thin layer of pale coral to her mouth. And I found one.

She was humming under her breath as she ran down

the stairs. She'd just reached the hallway when the doorbell sounded. She took a deep, calming breath and opened the door.

'Good morning,' she said. Her voice and expression were sedate, but her eyes were abrim with laughter and delight as she looked up at him.

Sam found he was catching his breath. He said a little hoarsely, 'How do you do that?'

'Do what?' Ros stood back to allow him into the hall, closing the door behind him.

'Make your mouth say one thing and your eyes something completely different.'

She flushed slightly. 'I—I didn't know I could.' He was wearing, she saw, close-fitting denim pants which accentuated his long legs, and a plaid shirt, both garments undoubtedly carrying designer labels. She said, 'You look—good.'

'You've stolen my line,' he said. 'Except that I was going to say—beautiful.'

She managed a small, rather choked laugh. 'I've never been that.'

'Yes, you have,' he said. 'You've never let yourself believe it, that's all. And perhaps you needed the right moment to blossom.'

She said hurriedly, 'Talking of blossoms—thank you for the roses. They're lovely.'

He looked at the vase on the mantelpiece, with its solitary bloom, and smiled. 'I saw that one had survived, and thought it looked lonely.' He added softly. 'I'm glad you kept it.'

Her blush deepened. 'I didn't—I mean—it was my cleaning lady. She's Spanish,' she added with a kind of desperation.

'Ah,' he said. 'Perhaps I should have asked her for a date instead.'

Ros laughed. 'She'd have turned you down. She's a happily married woman.'

'That's not always a guarantee of good behaviour.' He thought of Cilla Godwin's moistly parted lips, and his face hardened slightly.

She saw his expression change. She said quickly, before she could change her mind, 'Are you married, Sam? Or have you ever been?'

'God, no.' His reaction was too spontaneous to be anything but the truth. 'What gave you that idea?'

'I don't know.' She hesitated. 'I just get this—feeling that you're holding out on me in some way. That there are things about you that you don't want me to know.'

'You've forgotten our agreement,' he said, after a pause. 'A whole fresh start. Sam and Janie getting to know each other all over again.'

'It doesn't matter how much we pretend.' Her face was suddenly grave. She was speaking, she realised, to herself. 'We can never escape the people we really are.'

'But we can hide from them occasionally,' he said. 'And I know the perfect hiding place, especially on a day like this.'

'Let me guess.' It had been the right thing to say. Her smile reached out and touched him again. 'Somewhere by the river. Am I warm?'

He shook his head. 'You're not even tepid. And it's a surprise.'

The first part of the surprise was the car, an elegant Audi, parked a few yards down the road.

'I didn't know you drove,' Ros said, tucking herself into the passenger seat. 'I thought we'd be walking.'

'You see—the voyage of discovery has already begun. And I don't use the car a lot.' He paused. 'But at a time like this—a special time—it's convenient.'

She was scared of blushing again, so she frowned instead. 'But don't you need your glasses when you're driving?'

'Actually,' he said, 'I've decided I don't need them at all. Wearing them had simply become a habit. A failed attempt to make me look intellectual. Or something to hide behind,' he added.

She laughed. 'What have you got to hide from?'

'You'd be surprised.' He paused again. 'I thought you'd be glad to see the last of them.'

She gave him a thoughtful glance. 'Well—they never seemed quite right, somehow.'

Ros sat back as he negotiated the traffic on the Kings Road. He drove well, she thought. Positive without being aggressive.

Eventually she broke the silence. 'We seem to be heading out of London.'

'Well spotted.' He slanted a grin at her. 'I should have made you wear a blindfold.'

Her brows lifted. 'You know a brunch place out of town?'

'Not exactly. But I know a good picnic spot. Will you settle for that?'

She'd expected the safety of a busy restaurant. A secluded corner of the English countryside was a very different proposition. And he knew it as well as she did, she thought uneasily.

She swallowed. 'I'm not a great fan of alfresco dining.'

'There's an indoor option as well,' he said, worrying her even more. 'We can decide when we get there.'

'I suppose so.' Her hands, which had been lightly clasped in her lap, now seemed welded together.

'I made an early raid on the local deli,' he went on. 'We've got pâté, French sticks, olives, cold meat and Californian strawberries among other goodies.'

'It sounds—marvellous.' Ros forced a bright smile, then gasped as Sam suddenly pulled the wheel over and brought the car to a standstill at the side of the road.

He said, 'So what's the problem?'

'I don't know what you mean,' Ros defended.

'That's not true.' He shook his head, half reproving, half exasperated. 'In the space of a couple of minutes you've gone from relaxed and smiling to a fair imitation of a coiled spring. God, I can actually feel the tension in you from here. Why?'

There was a fleck on one of her nails. She examined it closely. 'Your change of plan has thrown me a little.' She attempted a laugh that broke in the middle. 'I don't think I'm very good at surprises.'

'Especially when they entail being alone with me? But you took that risk the first time we met.'

'That was a calculated risk,' she said. 'And I didn't intend to repeat it.'

'Yet you did,' he said. 'When I asked you. And here you are again now.'

'Yes,' she said. 'But for the last time—as we both know.'

'Of course.' He was silent for a moment. Then, 'Would it make any difference if I told you there was nothing to fear? That I swear I won't do anything that

you don't want. That I won't make a move—lay a
finger on you—without your permission—your invitation. Does that reassure you?'

He waited for a moment, then his voice hardened.

'Tell me, Janie, are you most scared of me—or
yourself? Be honest.'

She stared ahead of her through the windscreen, seeing nothing. She heard her voice shake a little. 'I don't
know. Is that honest enough?'

His tone was quiet. 'I guess it is.' There was another
brief silence, then he said with a touch of harshness,
'Look at me. Do it now.'

Ros turned her head reluctantly and met the piercing
turquoise gaze. Saw the cold set of the firm mouth.

He said, 'Shall I eliminate the risk factor? Turn the
car round and take you back to Chelsea and your safe,
comfortable life? Is that what you want?'

She only had to nod in acquiescence and it would
be done. She was sure of that.

And equally certain that, for better or worse, it was
the last thing she wanted to happen.

She found herself lifting her hand, brushing a finger
across that unsmiling mouth, hearing his sharply in-
drawn breath.

She said huskily, 'I'd like to go on.' Adding,
'Please.'

He captured her hand, held it while his teeth grazed
the soft pad of the marauding finger.

'Be careful,' he warned softly, as he released her.
'Because that might be construed in some circles as a
definite step on to the wild side.'

Ros let her eyes widen, the lashes veiling them provocatively. 'I was simply thinking of all that food. It
would be a crime to waste it.'

'By the time we get there,' Sam said, restarting the car. 'You should have quite an appetite.'

I think, Ros told herself, as she sank back into her seat, that I have one already.

'You might as well have blindfolded me,' she said half an hour later. 'I've no idea where we are.'

'You don't know this part of the world?'

'I don't know many places at all outside London,' she admitted ruefully. 'Except those I visit in connection with my work, of course.'

'Good,' he said. 'I'm glad I'm the first to bring you here.'

'So—where is "here"?' Not even the signposts meant much.

'It's not far now.'

It was turning into a heavenly day. The trees were vivid with new growth, and the lanes they were driving through were lush with cow parsley.

To Ros's pleasure, Sam put Delius's *Brigg Fair* on the car's CD player.

'I love this music,' she sighed. 'It's so incredibly English and romantic. I use it a lot when I'm working.'

'You use Delius to sell cosmetics?'

The astonishment in his voice alerted her to what she'd said, and Ros sat up, guilty blood invading her cheeks at her gaffe.

'Not exactly,' she said swiftly. 'I like to play it when I'm giving beauty treatments. It helps—relax the client.'

'It sounds wonderful.' He slanted a grin at her. 'Makes me wish I was beautiful.'

He would never be that, Ros thought. Not even if he grew his hair to a reasonable length. But those amazing eyes and the crooked smile which lit them to such devastating effect gave him the kind of attraction that transcended classic good looks.

This was a seriously sexy man, she told herself with bewilderment, and the last person in the world who needed to advertise for female companions. It was far more likely he had to beat them off with a stick.

Yet here we are, she thought. And I'm still wondering why. Although there's nowhere I'd rather be...

They drove across a narrow watersplash and into a picture-book village, with an ancient church and charming cottages, their walls washed in light pink, clustering round a central green.

This must be the picnic spot, Ros decided, surprised that he'd chosen somewhere public after all. The occupants of those houses wouldn't miss much.

But Sam was merely slowing for the turn, guiding the car up a narrow lane beside the church. Beside them, she saw a high brick wall, its lines softened by the clematis which was just coming into flower.

Sam turned in between two stone pillars and up a short, curving drive. The house at the end of it was also redbrick, simply and solidly built, and rather square, like a doll's house Ros had once possessed as a child. Above the porch, a wisteria was showing the first heart-stopping traces of blue, and there were climbing roses and honeysuckle trained round the windows.

'It's lovely,' Ros said, puzzled, as Sam parked outside the front door and retrieved a bunch of keys from the glove compartment. 'Is it yours?'

'No,' he said. 'I just know the owners.'

'Oh.' Relief fought with a kind of disappointment. He'd said nothing before about meeting his friends, although it was flattering—in a way—that he should want her to. And rather a nonsense, too, considering this was to be their final encounter.

It also occurred to her that she hadn't expected to share him.

She said breathlessly, 'They're very lucky to live here.'

'They don't,' he said. 'Or not much any more. They spend most of their time in the Dordogne. They bought an old farmhouse there a few years ago, and converted the barns into *gîtes*.' He swung his long legs out of the car and came round to open the passenger door. 'They're down there now, doing pre-season decorating and maintenance,' he said casually. 'So I thought I'd grab the chance to check the place over and sort out the mail.'

Ros managed another feeble 'Oh', swallowing past a sudden constriction in her throat. She paused. 'You're sure they won't mind—that you brought me with you?'

'I promise you,' he said, 'they'd be delighted. Now, wait a second while I deal with the security alarm, then I'll give you the guided tour.'

Ros stayed by the car, looking at the garden. It was worth savouring with its smooth lawns surrounded by wide borders just coming into flower. In the middle of the grass a stone bird bath was supported by a smiling cherub, and the entire expanse was surrounded and sheltered by the high wall.

'It's beautifully kept,' she said when Sam returned. 'Considering it's unoccupied.'

'A couple from the village look after it all,' he told her. 'Mrs Griggs cleans and her husband gardens. It's a perfect arrangement.'

The house itself was cosy and comfortable, with big squashy sofas and well-polished furniture which was a tribute to the efforts of the unseen Mrs Griggs.

The kitchen was mellow with antique pine, and a gleaming range, and there was an open fireplace in the sitting room with kindling and logs laid ready. There was also a baby grand piano, with a selection of music stacked neatly on its lid.

And, Ros saw, in pride of place, a photograph in a silver frame. The face was younger, and the hair longer, but the slanting smile was instantly familiar.

'This is you,' she accused, picking it up. She wheeled round on him. 'And you don't just "know" the owners. They're your parents—aren't they?'

'Guilty as charged,' Sam said ruefully. 'That's my graduation picture. I've never been able to persuade Ma to bury it somewhere.'

'But you said it wasn't your house.'

'Nor is it,' Sam returned promptly. 'It's where I grew up, and I have wonderful memories, but that's its only claim on me. I moved out and moved on a long time ago.'

'But surely...' Ros paused awkwardly. 'I mean it will be yours—in time.'

'No.' He shook his head. 'The parents are planning to move permanently to France, so it will be going on the market—probably this summer.'

'And you don't mind?'

'Not particularly.' His voice was amused. 'It's not a family heirloom. And you have to look forward, not to the past. And one day,' he added matter-of-factly, 'I intend buying a house of my own, so that I can create some good memories for my own children.'

There was a sudden roaring in her ears, and she

could feel the colour draining from her face, leaving only an aching emptiness behind.

From some vast distance, she heard herself say, 'Of course.'

And she turned back to replace the photograph on the piano with great care, terrified in case he noticed that her hands were shaking.

But he was walking past her to the French windows and opening them. 'Why don't you find us a picnic spot while I get the food ready?'

She nodded, and fled out into the open air, standing for a moment to draw great shuddering breaths as she fought for composure.

Because it had hit her with all the savage, overwhelming force of a tidal wave that there was only one woman she could bear to be the mother of Sam's children. And that was herself.

'No,' she whispered, gulping oxygen into her labouring lungs. 'No, this is ridiculous. It's not happening. I won't let it.'

Because she couldn't base a lifetime relationship on the strength of a few hours' dubious acquaintance. Or even casual lust. And that was all it was—however strongly her senses might be telling her otherwise. Even though they might be murmuring insidiously that in reality she had known Sam all her life—had breathed in the fact of his existence through her pores since the moment of her own creation. And had simply been waiting all this time for him to come to her.

Hormonal rubbish, she told herself crushingly. Janie's famous biological clock making itself felt.

Well, she would not allow it to control her perfectly satisfactory life. Particularly when, only a few weeks earlier, she'd been contemplating marrying a very different man with serenity, if not any great enthusiasm.

Hitching herself to the star of someone who advertised for company in a personal column had never been part of her plan.

In fact the whole thing had been a grotesque mistake from beginning to end.

I should never have got involved, she thought, forcing herself to walk along the flagged terrace. And if I'm going to suffer, it's entirely my own fault.

Which was no consolation at all.

And now she had to pull herself together and find somewhere for this picnic, when all she wanted to do was run away so far and so fast that Sam would never find her.

The terrace, she saw, taking her first proper look at her surroundings, had been constructed to overlook a small formal rose garden, and at one end there was a pergola, shaded by a lilac tree and containing a wrought-iron table and two chairs.

The lilac was just coming into bloom, and its faint, enticing scent drifted to her as a soft breeze curled through the branches.

For the rest of her life, she thought, the perfume of lilac would speak to her of love. And loss...

'So you've chosen my favourite place,' Sam said, arriving with a tray which he began to unload on to the table. 'I hoped you would.'

She said lightly, 'I think it chose me.' And felt her heart weep.

She wasn't hungry, but somehow she made herself eat, scared that Sam would notice and query her loss of appetite. And the food he'd provided was certainly worth sampling. As well as everything he'd mentioned, there were tiny spicy sausages, wafer-thin slices of Italian ham, wedges of turkey and cranberry pie, and sweet baby tomatoes, with a tall jug of Buck's Fizz to wash it all down.

Ros praised it lavishly, determined to keep the conversation going at all costs. For the first time in her life she was afraid of silence. Scared of what it might reveal.

And as she laughed and talked, her eyes were feeding a different kind of hunger. Memorising the distinctive bone structure of his face as if she was touching it. Watching his body language—the easy grace of his posture. The movement of his hands—the play of muscle under his shirt.

Each and every precious detail etched irrevocably into her mind to sustain her through the famine ahead of her.

He said at last, smiling at her, 'More strawberries?'

'I couldn't.' She leaned back in her chair, grimacing. 'As it is, I may have to start buying clothes with elasticated waists.'

He lifted an ironic brow, the turquoise gaze frankly appraising her slenderness, then lingering on the swell of her breasts under the creamy sweater.

He said gravely, his eyes dancing, 'I hardly think so. But if you really don't want anything else, I'll shift the debris indoors. I have a feeling the weather's going to change.'

Ros glanced up at the sky, and was startled to see heavy cloud, grey darkening to navy, massing in the west.

She thought, *'The bright day is done…'* And wondered what the dark would bring.

She pushed her chair back. 'Shall I help?'

'I can manage.' He began to load the tray. 'Relax, and enjoy the last remnants of sun while I put some coffee on.'

As he disappeared into the house, Ros got up and walked restlessly down the three shallow stone steps into the rose garden.

Not that there was much to see, except immaculately pruned bushes, but most of the roses were labelled, and she could use her imagination as she strolled down the gravelled path between the beds.

One sheltered corner had been planted with 'old' roses, and she bent down to read the beautiful, evocative names.

Sam said quietly from behind her, 'Rosamund,' and she jumped, whirling to face him, her lips parting in a startled gasp.

'How do you know? How did you find out?'

His brows snapped together in surprise. 'You can't escape knowing about roses if you live with my mother. And that one—Rosa Mundi—Rose of the World—is a favourite of hers. But I'm sorry if I frightened you,' he added with a touch of dryness. 'I thought you'd hear me.'

She bit her lip hard. 'I—I was in another world.' She gestured around her. 'How can she bear to leave all this? Her house, this garden—her roses?'

He said gently, 'She has another house, now, and another garden in the Dordogne, and they're beautiful too. And roses will grow anywhere. She'll simply plant more.' He put out a hand and touched her arm. 'God, you're trembling. I really did give you a shock. And you're like ice too.' His voice was remorseful. 'We'd better go inside.'

She moved away out of range. 'I'm fine.' She kept her voice light. 'Moving to another country is such a big step. What made them decide to do it?'

'My father's hobby has always been playing the stock market, and he made a hell of a lot of money from it back in the eighties.' Sam shrugged. 'They both love France, and nearly all our family holidays were spent there, so they got the idea of buying a house and doing it up. When Dad was offered early retirement it seemed like a golden opportunity to change their lives. So—they went for it.'

She gave a constrained smile. 'And that's where you get your financial skills.'

'Good God, no.' He laughed. 'I can barely add two and two.'

She stared at him. 'But you're an accountant.' She shook her head in amazement. 'An accountant who can't do sums?'

There was an odd silence. Then, 'Fortunately I have a calculator,' Sam said swiftly. 'And most of my work involves compiling reports anyway.'

She thought of her own accountant, and some of the things Colin had told her about his work.

She began, 'But surely....' And got no further. As if some gigantic hand had pulled an invisible plug, the rain came sheeting down with breath-snatching intensity, turning almost instantly to hail.

Sam grabbed her hand. 'Come on. Quickly.'

They ran for the steps, and back along the terrace, the hailstones bouncing around them, piercing their clothing with ice.

Sam thrust her ahead of him through the French windows, and turned to close out the storm.

Ros shook herself, freezing droplets spilling down from her drenched hair on to her face and shoulders.

She said, with a choked laugh, wrapping her arms round her shivering body, 'I'm absolutely soaking. My God—the joys of an English spring.'

She looked at him, expecting him to share her rueful amusement, and saw, instead, that he was watching her, his whole attention arrested, his eyes fixed almost blankly on the rain-darkened clothing clinging revealingly to her skin.

He said quietly, holding her gaze with his as he kicked off his shoes, 'Then maybe we should both get out of these wet clothes.'

And began to unbutton his shirt.

CHAPTER SEVEN

SHE could have stopped it right there, and she knew it. Because he'd promised as much. And he wasn't anywhere near her. He was—dear God—on the other side of the room.

But she didn't speak—or move. Just watched, in total sensual thrill, as he stripped off his shirt and let it fall. She let her eyes roam, hungrily absorbing the width of his shoulders, the brown hair-roughened skin.

The heavy silence in the room was broken only by the faint crackle of the wood he'd kindled in the hearth behind her, and by the harsh throb of her own breath. But maybe she was the only one who could hear it. Maybe—just maybe—his heart was hammering too.

She saw his hands move to the zip of his jeans.

She said swiftly, huskily, 'No—please.'

He paused as if turned to stone, the turquoise eyes sending her a challenge across the infinity of space that divided them.

He said, 'No?'

Hands trembling, she pulled off her sweater, dragging the mass of clammy wool over her head as if she could not wait another minute to be free. A second later her bra joined it on the floor.

She stepped out of her damp shoes and walked to him barefoot.

She said softly, 'Let me…'

She put her hands against his chest, feeling the flat male nipples harden at her touch, then allowed her palms to slide over the powerful ribcage to the flat, muscular stomach, where they lingered tantalisingly, her thumbs teasing the shadowed arrow of dark hair which pointed downwards, forcing a sharp, painful sound from his throat.

She leaned forward, brushing her lips against the wall of his chest, inhaling the potent male scent of him. Then, slowly, she released the single button at his waist and lowered the zip, easing the denim down from his hips.

Sam stepped out of the jeans, kicking them away. The briefs he was wearing did nothing to disguise the fact that he was already strongly and powerfully aroused. Ros stared at him, her eyes dilated, her mouth drying with excitement.

He whispered, 'Now it's your turn.' His hands were shaking as he unfastened her cream trousers and slipped them off.

He pulled her towards him, his hands stroking her naked back, making her gasp in startled pleasure. Instinctively her body arched in reply, and the swollen peaks of her breasts grazed against his chest. For a moment he held her there, moving his body slowly and rhythmically against hers, watching her nipples pucker with delight at the subtle friction.

He said huskily, 'They're like tiny roses. My rose of the world.'

Then he bent his head, and kissed her parted lips, his tongue seeking hers with aching, urgent sensuality. Their mouths clung, their teeth nipping delicately at the soft interior flesh.

The heated hardness of him was like a steel rod pressing against her thighs, and she felt her own fierce flood of moisture in response. A dark, feral scent seemed suddenly to fill her lungs. The scent of mating.

Her breasts were in his hands now, his fingers delicately strumming her nipples, raising their excitement to a new level and sending shafts of an almost unbearable sweetness piercing their way to her loins.

She moaned softly as Sam began to kiss her breasts, drawing each soft mound in turn deep into his hungry mouth, fondling their tautness with his tongue. His hands slid under the lacy briefs, gently moulding her buttocks, before initiating a more intimate exploration, his fingers paying tribute to the dark, wet heat of her surrender.

She was trembling wildly now, tiny golden sparks dancing inside her closed eyelids, as he discovered, then focused on one tiny pinnacle of pleasure, the throb of his caress sending ripples of pure arousal along her nerve-endings—creating the beginnings of a pleasure bordering almost on pain. But, however beguiling, it wasn't the fulfilment she sought. Her body was opening to him. Craving him in entirety.

'You.' Was that small, cracked sound her voice? 'Please—I want you. All of you.'

He said hoarsely, 'Yes.' And, 'Now.'

They sank together to the carpet, the final scraps of clothing hurriedly, clumsily discarded on the way.

For a brief moment she held him, then, with a tiny sob, guided him into her, and clasped him there.

He was still for a few seconds, allowing them both to savour this ultimate union of their bodies, then he began to move, his rhythm slow and powerful, and she echoed it, lifting her hips to meet each thrust, letting him fill her completely.

He whispered, 'Look at me, darling. I want to see your eyes when you come.'

'I—don't.' Her voice was muffled, breathless. 'Not—always.'

'That was then.' His hand slid down between them. 'This is—now.'

Her body imploded into rapture, every interior muscle contracting fiercely, sending liquid fire pulsing through her veins. She cried out, brokenly, ecstatically, and saw Sam rear up above her, his head thrown back, as the convulsions of his own climax tore through him.

They lay, their limbs still entwined, their sweat-dampened bodies joined together, waiting for the world to settle again, and their breathing to return to normal human limits.

His voice was muffled by her hair. 'Are you all right? I didn't hurt you?'

'No.' Her face was buried in his shoulder. She lifted her head and experimentally licked some of the salt from his skin. 'No,' she repeated as a small laugh was torn from her throat. 'You didn't do that.'

'I ask,' he said, his teeth nibbling gently at her earlobe, 'because—for a first time—that was pretty overwhelming.'

'I'd say it was perfect,' Ros corrected with mock hauteur.

'No,' Sam said with more firmness. 'It wasn't that. And never will be. Because "perfect" implies we don't need practice. And I know we do. Hours and hours of it.'

Her lips began to explore the hollow where his neck joined his shoulder.

'In that case,' she murmured, 'let's score it "average".'

'"Could do better"?' he suggested.

'If we live through it.' Ros moved slightly, preparing to detach herself, but his arms tightened round her.

'Keep still. Isn't it nice to lie like this?'

Another laugh shook her. 'It's—nice. But don't you need recovery time?'

'I have amazing powers of recuperation. Besides, it's a fact of nature. After the earthquake comes the aftershock. All we have to do is—wait.'

'That's all?'

'It won't be too dull,' Sam promised lazily. 'We can kiss each other—like this.' He turned her face towards him and caressed her lips softly with his. 'And I can play with your lovely breasts—like this.'

Ros ran her tongue along his lower lip. 'And I...' she whispered, as her hands cupped him intimately. 'I can do—this.'

'Oh, yes,' he said, gasping. 'You certainly can.'

She felt boneless. Boneless and weightless. So much so that without Sam's arm lying across her waist, anchoring her to the bed, she might have easily have floated up to the ceiling.

Sam had fallen asleep beside her, and she couldn't blame him. She was just aching, gently and pleasurably, but he had to be exhausted.

The aftershock had been slow and lingering, his hands and mouth making a feast of her, as if she'd been created simply and solely for his own very personal delight. He had taken her to the brink of rapture and held her there for some endless time, until her body had at last been permitted to splinter into orgasm.

She had come up to his room ostensibly to shower and dress, only to find him joining her in the tiled cubicle, his hands gently massaging shower gel into her shoulders and down the long, vulnerable sweep of her spine to her buttocks and thighs.

She'd stood under the torrent of warm water, hands pressed against the wall to steady herself, her senses tingling into a new and startled arousal as he'd parted her thighs and continued his intoxicating ministrations at a more intimate level.

Then he'd lifted her wet and slippery body into his arms and carried her out of the shower room, heedless of her breathless protests, to his bed.

This, she thought now, can't be happening to me.

Someone new—someone wanton—had crept inside her skin, and transformed her.

Sex with Colin had been conventional, but usually enjoyable, and often satisfying. Certainly she'd never had any real complaints.

But in Sam's arms she'd experienced another dimension. Learned wholly unsuspected truths about her body and the demands it could make. Discovered the delight of using her own hands and lips to give him pleasure.

She'd been sleeping with Colin for two years, but she'd known Sam's body more completely and intimately in a few hours.

She felt him stir drowsily beside her, and turned her head to look at him.

He said softy, 'So you're real. You're here. I was terrified you were still just a dream.' He found her hand and brought it to his mouth, pressing a kiss into her palm.

Faint colour stole under her skin. 'You're saying you've been dreaming about me?'

'Some of the time.' His eyes glinted at her. 'Most of it I couldn't sleep at all. Or work.'

'Nor could I,' said Ros, mentally crossing her fingers as she remembered her turquoise-eyed hero waiting for her in Chelsea.

My God, she thought. Is he in for a shock.

And found herself jumping as a door slammed somewhere downstairs and a woman's voice called out, 'Sam—Sam are you there?'

'Hell, it's Mrs Griggs.' Sam hurled himself off the bed and grabbed a robe. 'She must have come round to check up and seen the car.'

'You can't go down like that,' Ros protested. 'What will she think?'

'Hopefully, that I've been taking a shower.' Sam took a towel from the rail in his bathroom and rubbed his hair vigorously on the way to the door. 'Stay right here, darling.' His smile curled over her like a warm wave. 'I'll be back.'

Sighing, she leaned back against the pillows and waited, listening to the faint murmur of voices from the floor below. But the interruption had left her feeling suddenly restive.

The idyll, she thought, was over. Now it was back to the real world.

She swung her legs to the floor, and stood up. She was aware of all kinds of little aches and tender spots, but they were honourable wounds, she thought, with a small, private smile, and all in all she felt wonderful. On top of the world.

She really ought to get dressed, she thought, eyeing her clothes neatly draped across a radiator. But the lure of looking round Sam's room—the one he'd had since boyhood—was too strong. After all, weren't most of her misgivings centred around the fact that she knew so little about him? Well, this was a golden opportunity to find out. To put any lingering doubts to rest.

Not that the room gave much away. The decor was uncompromisingly masculine, with a stone cord carpet, and bedcover and drapes in olive-green. There were shelves of books, ranging from childhood favourites to modern novels, and a lot of non-fiction too, mostly to do with travel, and much of it centred in Africa, the Middle East and South America.

Presumably he kept the books and professional journals to do with his job at his London base, she thought, slightly puzzled.

There were no ornaments, and no pictures apart from two photographs—one of a good-looking middle-aged couple standing, smiling, with their arms round each other in front of some crumbling agricultural buildings. Presumably these were Sam's parents, pictured with the barns in the Dordogne, prior to conversion.

The other featured a golden retriever dog, who also seemed to be smiling.

She glanced along the shelves of books, recognising many titles she'd loved from her own childhood.

She pulled out a shabby copy of *The Wind in the Willows*, smiling as she recalled Ratty, Mole and Toad, and their adventures in the Wild Wood.

There was a bookplate in the front, with the name of a school on it. 'First Prize for English', it read. 'Awarded to S. A. Hunter'.

She stared down at it, frowning. Not Sam's book after all, she thought with odd disappointment. Then who…?

'What are you doing?'

She jumped violently in response to Sam's quiet voice from the doorway.

'Snooping.' She felt absurd, standing there naked, peering at books. She pushed *The Wind in the Willows* back on to its shelf. 'I thought these were yours.'

There was a slight hesitation. Then, 'Not all,' he said. 'I suppose, like most spare rooms once the children have moved out, this has become a bit of a dumping ground. Anyway,' he added with mock reproof, 'why aren't you waiting for me in bed, as specifically directed?'

'Because I think it's time we headed back to London, before any other neighbours come calling.' Rose paused. 'Did you manage to pull the wool over her eyes?'

'I was too busy keeping the wool over myself,' Sam said, tightening the belt of his robe as he walked towards her. 'She's a sweetheart, and I didn't want to shock her.'

His eyes were devouring her, already shadowy with desire.

Ros felt shy suddenly, and very undressed. She reached hurriedly for her clothes.

'I see it's stopped raining,' she remarked over-brightly, trying to reduce the situation to a more commonplace level, and aware that she was failing miserably.

'It stopped about two hours ago, but you were too occupied to notice.' Sam came up behind her, wrapping his arms round her and resting his chin on her shoulder. His warm breath caressed her ear.

'Why don't we forget about London and spend the night here?' he whispered. 'We can set off at the crack of dawn tomorrow.'

She could feel herself melting again. 'We can't...'

'Yes, we could.' His voice was husky. 'I want to sleep with you, Janie. To spend the whole night holding you in my arms. Don't you want that too?'

Janie. Whatever she might or might not want flew out of the window as her whole body stiffened.

Oh, God, she thought. Janie—who was coming back from Dorset late this evening. And who would expect to find her at the Chelsea house, alone and untouched.

She moved her head in swift negation. 'I—I have to get back. I have to work tomorrow.'

'Janie.' His voice held sudden urgency. 'Don't push me away again. Not after this.'

'It isn't that.' She turned in his arms, clasped his face between her hands and drew him down for her kiss. 'There are just—things I have to do.'

Like a stepsister to explain to, she added silently. A tissue of lies to unravel. Usual stuff.

'Tomorrow night, then.' The turquoise eyes were urgent—hungry. 'I'll cook you dinner at my flat.'

The wonder of the afternoon was shattering, splintering into tiny shards under the onset of reality.

She freed herself—stepped back—huddling her clothes clumsily in front of her. A gesture that was not lost on him, judging by his swift frown.

'Sam—' She tried to smile. 'This is all going too fast.'

'Janie,' he said, not smiling at all. 'You set the pace. And I didn't take anything you didn't want to give.'

'I don't deny that.' She bent her head. 'But it doesn't change a thing. You had a list. I was a name on it.'

'And now you're another notch on the bedpost. Is that what you're implying?' His tone was harsh.

She spread her hands, her eyes pleading. 'Sam—I don't know. After all, what do either of us really know about the other?'

And that, in spite of everything that had happened between them, was the real crux of the matter.

'I imagined today might have built up the database to some extent.' His smile was sardonic. 'I learned a hell of a lot.'

Her head lifted. She said crisply, 'That was sex.' And the most untrustworthy element in the universe...

'Really?' His brows lifted 'Now I could have sworn we were making love. I apologise for my gross error. It won't happen again.' He saw her flinch at the bite in his voice, but didn't soften. 'Get dressed, Janie, and I'll take you back. Just don't forget you were the one who wanted it this way.'

He stalked to the fitted wardrobe, pulled out jeans, a shirt and jacket, grabbed underwear from a drawer, and left the room, shutting the door hard behind him.

Ros trod over to the bed, and sank down on to the edge of it. She was trembling, and on the edge of tears. But she had to stay in control.

Everything had changed, she thought sombrely. Yet nothing had changed. She and Sam were still as far apart as they'd been when she'd first walked into that restaurant.

In fact, the glorious physical intimacy that they'd shared seemed to have stranded them at an even greater distance from each other. As if fate was tormenting her with a glimpse of what happiness could be like...

She wasn't some naive girl, who thought every bedroom encounter was a declaration of commitment or that being sexually compatible necessarily indicated an equal emotional stability.

But neither was she a risk-taker—someone who lived for the sensation of the moment. She thought she was a realist.

The happy endings she wrote about in her books were compounded from hope rather than experience.

Because sex was the great deceiver. It drew you in, sent you a little crazy, then spat you out.

It made you dream of—long for—impossible things. Plan for a future that only existed in your own imagination. Ignited all kinds of other emotions, like jealousy and suspicion.

She knew all that. Which made her behaviour of the past few hours even more inexplicable.

It had been realism which had tied her to Colin, she thought. The conviction that a relationship needed solid foundations in order to thrive and grow. That liking someone was safer than being head over heels in love.

And yet in less than a week Sam Alexander had blown all her carefully constructed theories to smithereens.

He had shown her more pleasure than she'd ever dreamed of. And opened the door to a pain that could leave her in total devastation.

That was the realisation she now had to live with.

Damn him, she thought, the muscles in her throat working convulsively. And more fool me for allowing it to happen.

And one of the most worrying aspects of the whole situation was that the Sam who'd pushed himself into her life and invaded her dreams no longer bore any resemblance to the wistful personal ad in the *Clarion*.

The emotive words about love and marriage had just been bait. She hadn't trusted them from the first. Yet, in spite of her disbelief, she'd been the one he'd caught in his trap.

How could I have done this? she asked herself bleakly. How could I have allowed it to happen? *Wanted* it to happen?

She stood. Made herself walk to the shower room and wash from head to foot, letting the water cascade over her head and shoulders, and down her trembling body. Then she towelled herself until her skin burned, before wrapping herself, sarong-style, in a dry bathsheet.

As she walked back into the bedroom, combing her damp hair with her fingers, Sam was standing by the bed.

Ros checked with a faint gasp, and saw his eyes turn to chips of turquoise ice as they scanned her.

He said curtly, 'Spare me the outraged virgin routine, Janie. We both know it's rubbish. Your having second thoughts doesn't suddenly turn me into a monster.'

'What do you want?' she demanded defensively. Anger seemed to surround him like a force field. She could feel its vibrations across the room, and had to resist an impulse to wrap her arms protectively round her body.

'Nothing that your over-heated imagination is suggesting.' His voice jeered at her. He held out her pair of cream suede loafers. 'I found these downstairs, that's all.'

She bit her lip. 'Oh—I'm sorry.'

'I don't think you know the meaning of the word.'

Stung, she threw back her head. 'And, you, of course, are some kind of saint.'

'No,' he said. 'But I'm honest with myself, at least, which is more than you can say, my sweet rose of the world.'

'Honest?' Her voice rose in scornful disbelief. 'Next you'll be telling me that personal ad was for real. So— was it, Sam? Were you genuinely looking for love and marriage? A relationship? For once, tell me the truth— if you can.'

He didn't look away, and she saw his face grow bleak and his mouth harden.

'No,' he said. 'None of it was true.'

'At last,' she said. 'Something I can believe.'

'Oh, cut the self-righteous indignation,' he came back at her grimly. 'Your reply to the Clarion ad wasn't exactly a model of candour either. Because you weren't "Looking for Love" at all. And you admitted as much.'

'Yes,' she said. 'But I had no ulterior motive. I—I did it for the best of reasons. Can you say the same?' She was shaking inside but she kept her voice steady. 'Which number was I, Sam? How many of the others who fell for your "Lonely in London" charade ended up in your bed? Tell me that.'

He tossed her shoes on to the bed. His voice was harsh. 'You're the first, Janie. And the last. However, you can believe what you want.'

He walked to the door. Paused. 'And while we're dealing with honesty, let's be brutal about it.' His glance skimmed her contemptuously. 'Because in spite of everything, I could have you out of that towel and back into bed, my warm and willing partner, for as long as I chose to keep you there. If I wanted to. You

know it, and I know it, so come down from the moral
high ground, darling. You're not fooling anyone.

'But as you're so hell-bent on getting back to
London,' he added curtly, 'oblige me by getting yourself into your clothes and downstairs in ten minutes,
or I'll come back and dress you with my own hands.'

His smile flicked her like the edge of a whip.

'Candid enough for you, darling?' he asked.
And went.

CHAPTER EIGHT

SHE had no one to blame but herself.

That was the thought that turned her brain into a treadmill during the silent, endless journey back to London.

It rained heavily all the way, and Sam, his face set in stone, drove with an unwavering, almost fierce concentration for which Ros could only be thankful.

She couldn't bear to hear any more, she thought wretchedly. She didn't want to be reminded of what a pathetic fool she'd been.

As they neared Chelsea, she said, 'You can drop me anywhere.'

'I'm taking you home,' he retired curtly, and she subsided, biting her lip.

There was a parking space right outside her house, and he slotted the Audi into it with icy precision.

As she fumbled with the door catch, Sam was out of the driving seat and round to the passenger side to open it for her.

'Thank you,' she said. By now, her lip was bleeding. The bitter, metallic taste filled her mouth. 'And goodbye.'

He ignored his dismissal and followed her up the steps. He held out a hand. 'Let me have your key.'

She began stiffly, 'There's really no need...'

'Another point we differ on. As you already know, I prefer to see you safely into the house.' He paused.

'And I'm not leaving until I've done it, so let's not waste time arguing.'

In seething silence, Ros handed him the key.

She stood defensively in the hall while he briefly checked the ground-floor rooms.

She gave him a small, wintry smile. 'However did I manage before I met you?'

'You didn't have to,' he said briefly. 'The security of the house was your parents' responsibility.' He paused. 'When are they coming back?'

'Two—three weeks.' Of course, she realised, he still thought this was their house.

He nodded, his face resuming the stony expression he'd worn in the car. 'I'll be in touch before then.'

'No.' The word was torn out of her. 'I don't want that. We said—you agreed...' She swallowed painfully. 'It ends here. Now. It must.'

'In spite of today?' His tone was curious—almost meditative.

'Because of today,' she flung at him. 'It should never have happened.'

'I can't disagree about that.' His mouth twisted wryly. 'But I'm afraid it's not that simple.'

'It was a mistake,' she insisted stubbornly. She paused. 'Or have I got it all wrong?' she added scornfully. 'Do I actually have to pay you to go away? Is that what it's all about?'

There was a terrible silence. As the turquoise gaze swept her, Ros felt as if she'd been suddenly encased in ice.

He said softly, 'Believe me, at this moment I'd give every penny I own and more to walk out of here and not look back. That was a cheap crack, Janie.'

She looked down at the carpet. 'I'm sorry,' she muttered. 'But you can leave. We—we don't have to compound the error. Make matters worse.'

He said quietly. 'Nature might do that for us. Unless you're on the pill, of course?'

Her lips framed another 'no' but no sound emerged. She stared at him—at this stranger standing in her own hall—saying the unthinkable. Warning her of the impossible.

She felt the colour draining from her face. Heard the sudden thud of her heart, panicking against her ribcage.

He nodded, his mouth set. 'In that case you and I have had unprotected sex. And that's why I'm staying in touch, and there's nothing you can say or do to stop me,' he added, between his teeth. 'Because if there are consequences, I want to know.'

He walked past her to the front door and paused, looking back at her.

She wanted to speak his name. Had a crazy yearning to say or do something that would bring him back to her. That would close his arms around her, keeping her safe.

But her mouth felt frozen. Her whole body seemed suddenly paralysed. She could only stare at him, her eyes enormous in her white face.

Because there was no safety any more. No security. And if she'd been capable of sound she would have howled like a dog.

He looked back at her, his mouth curling in a small, grim smile.

He said, 'I'll be seeing you.' And walked out, closing the door behind him.

She stood, leaning against the wall, staring unseeingly at the solid wooden panels of her own front door. The barricade that was supposed to keep out intruders. To protect her.

Except that of her own free will she'd jettisoned all her defences. Deliberately made herself vulnerable. Surrendered completely.

And now she might have to live with the consequences for the rest of her life.

I never even gave it a thought, she realised with a pang. Yet when I was with Colin, we always took precautions. Or he did.

Wanting Sam had filled her heart and mind to the exclusion of all else—including basic common sense, she thought, wincing. She'd been carried away on a riptide of emotion that had allowed for nothing but the total satiation of her senses.

She stirred restlessly. Being a fool was bad enough. She didn't have to make excuses. Nor did she have to be a victim, either.

It was time she stopped feeling sorry for herself and took control of her own life again, she thought with cold calculation.

So, she would call her doctor in the morning and ask to be prescribed the 'morning after' pill. Endure the lecture he would undoubtedly see fit to give her, and which she so richly deserved. And that would fix everything.

And then she'd be able to tell Sam that there was no need for him to bother any further. That the situation was taken care of. Write 'Finis' at the end of the chapter.

Except that she didn't actually know where to find him, she realised suddenly, and with horror.

Oh, God, she castigated herself. She'd been to bed

with this man—yet she didn't know his address, his telephone number, or even where he worked. The shame of it left her reeling. Not to mention the unmitigated stupidity.

She'd have to keep that from the doctor, she thought feverishly or he'd send her to see a psychiatrist. And who could blame him?

She began to walk towards the stairs, and paused, rigid with a new fear as she heard the sound of stealthy movement on the floor above.

Sam hadn't simply been playing the dominating male when he'd checked the house, she thought, drymouthed. There'd been a genuine danger which he'd been aware of but she hadn't. Until now—as all the statistics she'd ever read about women being attacked in their own homes rose up to haunt her.

She backed down the hall, reaching with damp, clumsy fingers for the telephone, only to see a yawning Janie appear on the half-landing.

'Oh God.' Ros drew a deep, shaky breath. 'It's you. You—you startled me.'

'Of course it is. Who else were you expecting?' Janie ran her fingers through her hair, peering down at Ros. 'Where on earth have you been?'

'I went out.' Ros forced herself to smile, to attempt to speak normally. 'I wanted some fresh air. It—it was such a lovely day,' she added lamely.

'Lovely?' Janie echoed incredulously. 'Are you kidding? We've had inches of rain, plus thunder and lightning. I took a couple of paracetamol as soon as I got in, and fell asleep on the bed.' She paused. 'Are you on your own? Because I could have sworn I heard voices. That's what woke me.'

'It was just the answering machine.' Ros took a

deep breath. 'What are you doing back here so early anyway?'

Janie tossed her head. 'I got Martin to bring me home. I couldn't stand any more of his mother clicking her tongue and saying we were in too much of a rush over the wedding. She kept looking me up and down, trying to suss out if I was pregnant, the dirty-minded old bat.'

Ros sighed inwardly. 'I thought you liked his parents.'

'I bent over backwards to like them,' Janie declared moodily. 'But they clearly don't think I'm good enough for their beloved son.'

In spite of her inner turmoil, Ros's lips twitched. 'There's a lot of it about,' she agreed, gravely. 'But I might have reservations too if a child of mine suddenly rolled up with someone I'd never heard them mention before, saying they were engaged.'

'Oh, I might have known you'd take their side.' Janie's tone was pettish.

'I'm not taking sides at all,' Ros assured her wearily. 'I wouldn't dare.' She paused. 'Are there any paracetamol left? Because I'm actually developing quite a headache myself.'

'Really?' Janie sent her a frowning glance. 'To be honest, darling, you do look like hell. As pale as a ghost. Your day out doesn't seem to have done you much good.'

'I was just thinking exactly the same thing,' Ros said with tired irony, and went upstairs to her room.

She wanted to sleep. To close her eyes and sink into blessed oblivion. But she couldn't relax. Her churning brain wouldn't allow it. Nor would her heightened emotions, prodded into turmoil by a host of unwanted memories.

Because Sam was with her—in this house, this room, this bed—and there was no escape from him. She could taste his skin, sense its texture beneath her seeking hands. She could feel the warm weight of his body grazing hers. The silken hardness of him filling her. The joy of him, and the unbelievable, unceasing pleasure.

She pressed a clenched fist against her trembling lips to repress a moan.

She had to do something to rid herself of this torment, she thought desperately. To exorcise this ghost who lay with her and whispered words of passion and desire that she dared not hear.

With sudden resolution, she swung her feet to the floor, reaching for a robe, catching sight of herself in the long wall mirror as she did so.

She paused and was still, observing herself closely and painfully. Searching for visible changes in the body she'd thought she knew so well, and which no longer, in some strange way, seemed to belong to her. Which might, already, be possessed by someone else.

A little quiver ran through her senses. She straightened her back, feeling the faint pull of her aching muscles, the voluptuous tenderness of her breasts.

Impossible, she thought wonderingly, that she should look no different. Yet the slim figure confronting her appeared the same. There were no bruises, she acknowledged wryly. No obvious scars. For a second her hand touched the flatness of her stomach, in a gesture that was pure question, then she realised what she was doing and snatched it away.

It's my heart that's changed, she thought sadly. And my mind. The other—well, that isn't even an option.

She put on her robe and tied the sash tightly, then went barefoot up to her study.

After all, she reasoned, as she switched on the computer, she'd been able to exploit the excitement and sexual tension she'd enjoyed in Sam's company. Now she could use the pain too, if that was all there was left for her.

She was still working two hours later, when Janie put a surprised head round the door.

'I thought you were asleep. I came up to tell you I've put a Spanish omelette together, if you'd like some.'

'Thanks.' Ros smiled at her, flexing weary shoulders. 'That's really thoughtful, love.'

'Oh, well.' Janie gave an off-hand shrug. 'Actually, I need to talk to you, Ros. To ask your advice.'

Ros bit her lip as she got to her feet. 'I'm the last person who should be advising anyone,' she said bleakly. 'My life isn't a conspicuous success at the moment.'

'How can you say that?' Janie led the way downstairs to the kitchen. 'You have your career—this marvellous house. Even a man—of sorts.' She pulled a face. 'Where is Colin, by the way? I thought he'd be back from his rugby tour by now and well ensconced.'

'Actually, no.' Ros tried to sound casual as she sat down. The omelette, which Janie dished up from the pan with a flourish, smelt wonderful, crammed with ham, peppers, tomatoes and cheese. She picked up a fork. 'Colin and I are no longer an item.'

'My God.' Janie's eyes were like saucers. 'Maybe

I should go away more often. You could transform your entire life.'

Ros forked up some omelette. She thought, I'm afraid I already have...

'So what prompted this?' Janie demanded eagerly.

Ros shrugged. 'It just—seemed the thing to do,' she returned evasively.

'Hmm.' Janie gave her a narrow-eyed look as she filled two glasses with Rioja. 'A likely story. My guess is that you've met someone else. And now you're blushing,' she added gleefully. 'Come on—tell me everything.'

Ros said crisply, 'You have a vivid imagination, Janie. There's—no one.'

Janie pouted slightly. 'Well, maybe you have a point. I'm still not sure that Martin's the right man for me. Not if he won't stand up for me against his parents.' She sighed. 'It's all a bit of lottery, isn't it? Perhaps I should have stuck to my plan and met "Lonely in London" after all.'

Ros's fork clattered on to her plate. 'No,' she exclaimed, too quickly.

Janie stared at her. 'How do you know?' Her face was suddenly wistful. 'He could have been the man of my dreams.'

'Possibly,' Ros said coldly. 'And you'd be just another conquest for a serial womaniser. Something for him to brag about with his friends.'

Janie tossed her head. 'Well, there's no need to get so het up about it. After all, I gave him the brush-off, thanks to you. I don't suppose I'd get a second chance, even if I wanted one.'

Ros reached across the table and took her hand. 'Promise me you won't try,' she said urgently.' I'm sure things will work out with Martin in the end—if you want them to—and you're prepared to compromise. But if not you'll meet someone else, Janie. I know you will. But not through some ghastly cheating, lying advertisement,' she added passionately.

There was a pause, then, 'Wow.' Janie gave an uncertain laugh. 'You sound as if you really mean that.'

Ros nodded, her heart as heavy as a stone in her chest. 'Believe it,' she said. And went back to her supper.

One day followed another in bleakness. Ros worked crazy hours, ensuring that when she went to bed she was too tired even to dream.

She went to the doctor, listened to his strictures about prevention being better than cure, obtained her prescription, and then walked, without the slightest hesitation, straight past the pharmacy. When she got home, she locked the slip of paper into a drawer in her desk.

My secret talisman, she mocked herself.

The book, however, began to go well, and by the end of the week she had enough to show Vivien.

She sat tensely, watching the older woman scanning the lines of script, her fingers rapidly turning the pages.

When she'd finished, Vivien said, 'Keep this up and it will be the best thing you've ever done.' She laughed. 'It's a total transformation. What's happened to you?'

Ros thought, I fell in love. And forced herself to smile.

It was raining when she came out of the publishing office. Cursing under her breath, she turned up her collar, tucked her briefcase under her arm and scurried up the road to the intersection to look for a taxi.

She managed to hail one at last, but, to her fury, a man further up the street leapt out of a shop doorway and collared it.

'I hope your tyres burst,' she hurled after it, realising, even before she'd finished speaking, that another vehicle was drawing up at the kerb beside her.

She turned gratefully, and saw it was indeed a black car. But not a black cab.

All the breath in her body seemed to leave in one shocked, painful gasp as she recognised the Audi.

Sam leaned across and opened the passenger door. 'Get in,' he directed curtly.

'No way.' She almost spat the words. 'I'll walk.'

'You'll drown.'

'My exact choice.' Head high, she started off down the street, going in entirely the wrong direction, she realised with chagrin.

She heard the Audi's door slam, and the purr of its engine as it cruised along beside her, making a mockery of her hurrying steps.

Sam spoke to her through the open window. 'Don't make this a problem, Janie. We're starting to hold up the traffic.'

To her annoyance, she saw that, because there were vehicles parked on the opposite side of the road, a van and two other cars were indeed already waiting behind the Audi, with clearly mounting impatience.

As she hesitated, the van driver leaned out of his own window. 'Do us all a favour, girlie, and get in for Gawd's sake.'

The Audi's door opened again, and, face flaming, Ros took the passenger seat.

'This is harassment,' she accused, fumbling with the seat belt. 'Have you been following me?'

'No.' Sam took the metal clip from her and slotted it neatly into place. 'I just happened to be in the neighbourhood.'

'Really?' Her tone was sceptical. 'Doing what, precisely?'

'Visiting a friend in hospital.'

She did not look at him. 'You surprise me.'

'Why? Because I have a friend?' There was an edge to his voice. 'Or because you've given me a compassion rating of zero?'

'Those are both good reasons,' she said. 'But principally because it's an odd time of day to be paying visits. You must have a very lenient boss. That is, of course, if you actually do work at all.'

'Ah, yes,' he said softly. 'At our last meeting you credited me with a career as an extortionist. How could I forget?'

'You obviously have a very poor memory,' she said. 'I also made it plain I didn't want to see you again.'

'And I told you with equal frankness that we were stuck with each other,' he came back at her grimly. 'At least for a while, anyway. So why not graciously accept a ride home?'

Her lips parted incredulously. 'You expect—you want me to be gracious?'

'It wouldn't be my primary option,' Sam returned coolly. 'But beggars can't be choosers. So, I'll settle for what I can get. Even if it's a fit of sulks,' he added, shooting a lightning glance at her defensively hunched shoulder.

'I'm supposed to be pleased that you've—hijacked me in a public street?'

He shrugged. 'No more than I'm glad to have you dripping all over the inside of my car. Let's say they're just—necessary evils.' He paused. 'And as a matter of interest what are you doing in this area? It's hardly the hub of the cosmetics industry.'

'I had a professional appointment,' Ros said coldly. 'If it's any of your concern.'

One moment, they were in an orderly line of traffic. The next, Sam had spotted a gap in the adjoining lane and dived across it and down a quiet side street, where he stopped.

He turned to look at her, the turquoise eyes blazing. He said slowly, 'I can think of circumstances which would make it very much my concern. I've just come from a private clinic. It happens to specialise in cardiac cases, but there are plenty of others round here with very different purposes.'

'Others?' Ros echoed, and then realised. She said, with a little gasp, 'I don't even know if I'm pregnant. Not yet.' She lifted her chin. 'If you got me into this car looking for reassurance you're going to be disappointed.'

She paused. 'But when—if,' she corrected hurriedly, 'I discover it's true, that will be the time for making decisions.'

And tried not to think about the unfilled prescription in the locked drawer.

He said quietly, 'I hope I may be consulted before you finally decide—about anything. Will you promise me that?'

Her throat closed. She said huskily, 'It's my body.'

'But our child.' The reminder was softly spoken, but it struck Ros to the heart.

As he restarted the car, she turned and stared out of

the passenger window at the blur of buildings and traffic.

But whether her view was distorted by the rain or by the tears she was fighting to control was a question she could not answer.

CHAPTER NINE

WHEN the car eventually stopped, Ros was still too immersed in her unhappy thoughts to take much note of her surroundings. Accordingly, she was already out of the car and heading across the pavement before she registered that Sam had parked in front of a small block of flats in a street that bore no resemblance to her own Chelsea base.

She swung round to find him locking the car. 'What the hell is this? What's going on? You offered me a lift home.'

'This is home,' he said. 'My home—at least for the time being. I thought you'd like to see it.'

'Then you thought wrong.' She drew a quick, sharp breath. 'Where's the nearest tube station?'

'About a quarter of a mile away.' He pointed out the direction with a casual gesture. 'A brisk and very wet walk. Alternatively, you can stop being bloody-minded, come up with me, and have some coffee or a drink while we wait for the rain to pass. But make your mind up quickly, please. I'm not in the mood for pneumonia.'

She should have turned and gone instantly. Her hesitation had been fatal, and she knew it. She lifted her chin and walked through the double glass doors he was holding open for her.

They rode up in the lift in silence. Ros stood rigidly, her arms folded across her body, looking anywhere but at him. Knowing that he was watching her, and that she didn't want to read the expression in his eyes. Did not dare to.

She waited as Sam unlocked a door on the second floor and stood aside for her to precede him. 'Welcome,' he said with faint mockery.

'If you say so.' One swift appraisal told her plenty. It was a large flat, clean and comfortable, but totally masculine in ambience.

Apart from a couple of photographs, the interior was workmanlike—almost Spartan. There weren't many personal touches at all, but maybe that was deliberate.

In fact, it was more like an office than home. Or a staging post for someone always on the move. It had a strangely transient air, she thought, recalling the travel books at the other house. As if the occupier were simply—passing through.

If any women had stayed there they'd left no traces of their tastes or personalities. Or perhaps they just hadn't been around for long enough...

'Well?' There was still that underlying note of amusement in his voice.

She paused. 'You're very—tidy.'

'Not always,' he said. 'My mother would say I haven't been back here long enough to create any serious mess. Besides, I always make an effort when I'm expecting visitors.'

'You were expecting—me?'

'I was counting on it.'

She lifted her chin. 'So, you were following me after all.'

'No,' he said. 'I told you. I was visiting a friend in the Albermarle Clinic. He's recovering from a mild heart attack and is due to be discharged quite soon, when his wife is going to whisk him off to a quiet village in Yorkshire to recuperate. Now you know it all.'

He paused. 'Anyway, I didn't have to follow. Because I knew I'd find you And I wouldn't even have to go looking.'

Ros shrugged. 'You make it sound important.' Her voice was dismissive.

'And so it is—to me.' He walked into the kitchen, filled the kettle and plugged it in while she watched from the doorway. He sounded almost reflective. 'You see, I've got tired of being dumped outside your door like a bag of trash each time you have second thoughts.'

He smiled at her. 'So I decided, for a change, that you could come here, and we could be together and talk, until we had the inevitable big row, when I could kick you out instead.'

It was not funny, Ros told the silence that followed in outrage. It simply was not. This was the man who'd destroyed her peace of mind and turned her life to turmoil.

So why did she feel laughter welling up inside her, eventually emerging in a small, uncontrollable wail?

She found herself clinging to the doorpost, over-whelmed by a tidal wave of giggles, unable to speak, barely able to breathe, tears running down her face.

Only to realise, suddenly, that she was no longer laughing, but weeping, her giggles replaced by sobs that tore at her throat.

Sam was across the kitchen at her side, his arms enfolding, his voice suddenly, magically soothing. She let her shaking body sink into his embrace, pressing her face convulsively into his shoulder, and felt his hand gently stroking her hair.

At last, her sobs still shuddering through her, she lifted her head and tried to speak. To apologise? To make some plea? She would never be sure.

He shook his head, and touched a finger lightly to her lips, forbidding speech. Then he began to kiss her, swiftly, lightly, his mouth brushing the tears from her lashes and drenched cheeks.

Only it wasn't enough, some drowning part of her recognised. She wanted more. She wanted everything.

Her hands reached up, gripping his shoulders with fierce intent. She stared up at him, her lips parting—trembling...

She heard Sam give a soft, muffled groan, then his mouth covered hers in a demand as deep and unashamed as her own.

She answered it with something that bordered on delirium, savouring the taste of his mouth, the thrust of his tongue, scalding hot and honey-sweet. The kiss clung, broke for the beat of a breath, then raged again, enflaming and engulfing them both.

Ros tipped her head back, letting his lips slide down the line of her throat, feeling the subtle flick of his tongue around the hollow of her ear.

His hands cupped her breasts, moulding them through the ribbed silk of her sweater, and she gasped, arching her body so that the delicate peaks thrust in mute offering against his caressing fingers.

He pushed roughly at her sweater, his fingers freeing the clasp of her bra so that his lips could feed on the untrammelled, scented roundness that he had released.

She encircled his head with her arms, holding him to her, glorying in the bittersweet tug of his mouth on her flesh.

His hands grasped her hips, pulling her body forward so that it ground against his, male and female in the eternal heated conjunction.

Her legs were shaking, her body melting as he lifted her into his arms and carried her away.

As he lowered her she felt the softness of a mattress under her back, and the scent of fresh linen.

Then Sam knelt over her, hands clumsy with haste as he began to rid her of her clothes, and she was aware of nothing else but him. There was no sound in the room now except the rasp of fastenings and the rustle of discarded fabric, combined with the harsh urgency of their breathing.

Naked at last, they came together, his fingers stroking her exquisitely to flame, to prepare her for the first stark thrust of possession. He entered her without hesitation, and her hips lifted eagerly to meet him, her legs locking round him, her hands clinging to his sweat-damp shoulders.

Staring down at her, eyes half closed, the muscles knotted in his throat, Sam drove into her, deeply, rhythmically, and her body rose in response, drawing him further and further into some molten infinity of need.

At the very edge of consciousness, Ros was aware of the first dark stirrings of pleasure unfurling slowly and inexorably within her.

Even as she cried out silently, It's too soon. Not yet... she was overtaken. Overwhelmed. Left spent and shaken, hearing her voice uttering its last moans of voluptuous delight.

Hearing Sam groan in turn, as he reached his own extremity of sensation.

And this time the tears he kissed from her face were tears of joy.

A long time later, she said, 'So this is your bedroom.'

'You don't miss much.' She heard the grin in his voice, and her own mouth curved.

'I didn't get much chance to admire the decor,' she reminded him, dropping a kiss on his shoulder.

He rested his cheek on her hair. 'Now you'll tell me that the ceiling needs painting,' he murmured, and yelped as she bit him softly. 'So—do you approve?'

Without moving from his arms, Ros took a leisurely look round. A plain stone-coloured carpet, she noted, complemented by a classic wardrobe and tallboy in some dark polished wood, navy curtains at the window, and bedding in navy and white percale.

'It looks good,' she said. 'Subdued.'

Sudden laughter shook him. 'What were you expecting—mirrors on the ceiling—black satin sheets—hidden video cameras?'

'I didn't know what to expect,' she said. 'Maybe that's what worries me. Here we are—and yet I know so little about you, Sam. So very little.'

There was a silence, and she felt the chest muscles beneath her cheek tense slightly.

He said, 'That's why I brought you here. So you could see that I have a place to live, and I'm not existing out of a cardboard box on the street. To prove to you that I live alone too.'

He paused. 'And it's not part of some lonely hearts ploy either—before you ask. I've brought no one else here. You're the first.'

She said in a small voice, 'Oh.'

'Is that "Oh, I'm pleased" or "Oh, I'm sorry"?'

'I—I'm not sure.'

He said quietly, 'Do you feel it's all moving too fast for you?'

'I think that's what I ought to feel.'

'But?'

Her fingers strayed across his chest, stroking the flat nipples. She said slowly, 'But it's difficult to believe you haven't always been part of my life.'

He nodded. 'I have something to confess too.' He put his hand under her chin, tipping up her face so that he could look into her eyes. 'I said earlier that I wouldn't have to go looking for you, but it was a lie. I was actually on my way over to your house when I saw you.

'And it wasn't to find out whether or not you're pregnant, either,' he added huskily. 'It was because I couldn't bear to keep away any longer.'

'So it must have been fate,' she said. 'Do you believe in fate?'

'I never did before.'

He kissed her, his mouth moving gently, languorously, on hers.

When her breathing steadied, she said, 'I might not have opened my door to you.'

'I was prepared to take that risk,' he said. 'And I'd have camped on your steps and sung you love songs until you had to let me in. Because I have this really terrible voice.'

A little quiver of laughter ran through her, followed by a deep shudder of anticipation because his hand was moving, slowly but very surely, caressing the tautening swell of her breast, then moving downward to stroke the silken skin of her thigh, before seeking once more the inner heated moisture it protected.

Reducing her in seconds to gasping, molten sensation. A state of exquisite, pulsating chaos where nothing mattered except his lips, his fingers, and the hard strength of his body invading hers—possessing her utterly.

Afterwards, she fell asleep in his arms. But at some point he must have eased himself away from her, because when she woke she was alone in the bed.

Ros propped herself up on an elbow and stared round the empty room. She was just beginning to feel uneasy when the door opened and Sam came in. He was dressed, she saw, casual in jeans and a white cotton shirt, and he was carrying two beakers of coffee.

'I bet the first thing Sleeping Beauty asked for after the prince's kiss was room service,' he remarked, putting the coffee down on the night table.

'Wrong.' Ros pushed her hair back ruefully. 'It was a mirror.'

'We have those too.' His lips touched the top of her head. 'But you look quite beautiful enough, so drink your coffee first.'

Faint colour rose in her face as she sat up, pulling the sheet around her body.

'You're going shy on me again,' Sam lounged on the end of the bed, his eyes disconcertingly intent as they studied her. 'Don't you think that's locking the stable door after the horse has not simply bolted, but vanished over the horizon?'

'I suppose so.' Her colour deepened. 'But this is the way I am. I—I'm sorry.'

'Don't be,' he said. 'I like the way you are.'

She paused. 'I thought you'd be sleeping too. Are you some kind of superman?'

'Far from it,' he said, and paused. 'But I had some heavy-duty thinking to do,' he went on levelly. 'And I think better without a naked and very desirable girl in my arms.'

The coffee scalded her throat, making her gasp. 'Experience has taught you that?'

'No,' he said. 'Some delayed but necessary common sense.'

'Common sense?' Ros echoed, keeping her voice light. 'I don't think I like the sound of that.'

'I felt one of us should try it—however late in the day.' He was silent for a moment. 'I want you to know that when I brought you here I didn't intend—any of this.'

His mouth tightened. 'If I had done, I might have been—better prepared,' he added with rueful emphasis.

She tried a smile. 'What were you just saying about a bolting horse?'

'That's the whole point. We made one serious mistake already.' His own expression was sober—almost grave. 'We didn't have to compound it today. And for that I blame myself totally. We've been playing a kind of sexual Russian Roulette—and it has to stop.'

In spite of the coffee's heat, there was a sudden cold feeling in the pit of Ros's stomach.

She found herself examining the pattern on the beaker rather too carefully. 'There's no question of blame,' she said quietly. 'We both wanted this—didn't we?'

'Yes,' he said. But that still doesn't make it right.'

'No,' she said. Fright stirred and shook inside her. 'No, of course not.'

There was another silence, then he said bluntly, 'All this has happened at a bad time for me, Janie. My life's a mess. I have to get it sorted.'

And move on. He didn't say it, but she heard the words in her head. He'd been abroad, he'd come back, and soon he would be gone again. All the clues to his life were there, just waiting to be recognised. And staying around—commitment—was not part of his agenda.

I noticed, she thought with anguish, *but I didn't build up the pattern. I didn't realise this had 'temporary' written all over it. Not until this moment.*

Hurt made her want to hit back. She said, 'I happened at an inconvenient time for you. You happened at a convenient time for me. I guess we cancel each other out.'

'Convenient?' His brows drew together sharply. 'What the hell are you talking about?'

'I was having problems with my boyfriend,' she said. 'I'm sure I told you. Well—since I haven't been available—he's been coming round again. Phoning me. Suggesting that we should give ourselves another chance.'

He was very still. 'And shall you?' he spoke evenly.

'I don't know yet.'

'Of course you don't.' His tone bit. 'A second chance with another man's child thrown in might be a little much for him.'

'I—don't think that will happen.'

'How can you be sure?'

Because I'd know if I had your baby inside me, beginning its life, she wanted to scream at him.

Because I'd feel it there, in every fibre of my being. My body would be a haven—a secure place, warm, dark and hidden—instead of a scared, disintegrating shell...

She shrugged. 'Instinct, I suppose.'

'A very potent thing. And how are his antennae working, I wonder?' He was smiling, but his eyes were blazing. 'Will they pick up that you're not the same person any more? Tell him that you've spent hours in bed with someone you hardly know?'

Ros put the beaker down on the night table. 'I can't believe we're having this conversation.'

'I'm simply trying to make you understand that you don't want him. That you don't need to say these things, because I'm being punished enough already. But you can't involve someone else in our private war. It isn't fair...'

'Don't talk to me about fair.' Her voice shook. 'You haven't been fair with me from the start. Well, have you?'

Deny it, she pleaded inwardly. Oh, please deny it. Say that I'm imagining things. Tell me you want me—that we have a future together some day—and I'll believe you. I swear I will...

He bent his head. His voice seemed to come from the far side of the room. 'No,' he said. 'No, I haven't.'

There was a silence, and pain poured into it. Filled it, so that she could not breath, or think, or speak.

'Janie,' he said. 'Look at me. Accept that I won't offer promises or guarantees that I might not be able to keep.' He took a deep breath. 'You don't know how much I'd like to say "Live with me and be my love", but I can't. Not the way things are. And under the circumstances I had no right to bring you here—to make love to you again. Only don't ask me to regret a minute of it. Because I can't, and I never will.'

'Is that supposed to make everything all right?'

'No,' he said. 'That would be asking too much.'

She stared at the stitching on the coverlet. 'Is it another woman? Is that the "mess" you have to sort out?'

'No.' The word exploded from him. 'At least, not in the way that you mean. But don't ask me to explain any more—at least not now.'

'You don't have to explain—or apologise. Not now. Not ever. You didn't force me. My God.' She gave a small, brittle laugh. 'You barely had to seduce me. We're both consenting adults, and there are no broken bones. These things happen.'

'Not,' he said softly, 'in the way that they happened to us.'

She said, 'There is no "us".' And swallowed. 'Could you leave me alone now, please? I'd like to get dressed.'

It was a ludicrous request, when they both knew there wasn't an inch of her that he hadn't explored with his hands and lips. He could probably have sketched her from memory.

She expected at the very least some jeering remark, even if he didn't laugh in her face.

Instead, he nodded silently, and left the room.

Ros huddled into her clothes. She felt numb—empty now. But that wouldn't last. The pain would return, and this time it could destroy her.

In the two years she'd spent with Colin she'd never glimpsed the depth of emotion she felt for Sam after only a matter of days.

How cruel that was, she thought desolately, and

how unjust. Colin had deserved so much better. He'd always been loyal and decent. She'd been the one who'd held back, reluctant to commit herself.

And now, like a pathetic idiot, she'd mistaken a few hours of white-hot passion for love. Chosen a man who'd only wanted sex without complications, and was now backing away.

Humiliation clawed at her. She'd meant to be cool and careful, but she'd let him see too much of her hopes and needs. She'd opened the door and allowed him into her heart—into the centre of her being.

Now she had to get out of here with as much self-respect as she could salvage.

He was speaking on the phone in the living room. She longed to be able to creep past to the front door and make her escape while he was still engaged on his call, but she'd left her bag and briefcase by the sofa and she couldn't leave without them.

So she lifted her chin and squared her shoulders, and walked into the room.

Sam was replacing the receiver. He was frowning, lost in thought, then he looked up and saw her, and time seemed to stop as they looked at each other. His expression was set, the turquoise eyes unfathomable.

Ros controlled a shiver.

She said, 'I came for my things.'

She saw a muscle move beside his mouth. 'Yes, of course.' He paused. 'I'll drive you home.'

'No,' she said. And again, 'No—thank you. I'll get a cab.'

'As you wish.' His voice chilled her. 'Then I'll find one for you.'

They rode the lift down in silence, standing on opposite sides of the metal cage.

The rain had stopped, but the air smelt dank and forbidding as they emerged on to the street.

Sam saw a cruising taxi in the distance and hailed it.

As it approached, he said quietly, 'Is there any point in my asking you to be patient—to trust me?'

'None.' Some miracle kept her voice level. 'It's over. Finished.'

She saw sudden colour burn along his cheekbones. He said softly, 'Like hell it is.' And reached for her.

His kiss was hard and angry, plundering her mouth ruthlessly. She felt the burn of it deep in her bones, and, through all the rage and hurt, the tiny coil of response and arousal that she was powerless to forbid.

When he let her go, she stepped back with a gasp, putting a hand mutely to her swollen lips.

'Something to remember me by.' He was breathing rapidly, and his smile glittered at her. 'Until we meet again.'

'All hell,' she said hoarsely, 'will freeze over first.'

Voice shaking, she gave her address to the clearly fascinated driver, and almost threw herself into the back of the cab.

As they drove off, something told her that Sam was still standing there, watching her go.

But she did not turn her head to check. Pride, she told herself, would not allow her to do so.

And besides, she realised with sudden devastation, she could be wrong. And that would be the worst thing of all.

CHAPTER TEN

YOU fool, Sam denounced himself savagely as he watched the cab pull away. You stupid, criminal bastard. Why the hell didn't you tell her the truth—the whole miserable story—from day one?

Because you were scared—that's why. You were afraid to tell her everything in case you lost her. And now you've lost her anyway.

He supposed he'd been hoping wildly that he could emerge from the situation with some kind of honour, but he suspected he'd been praying for the impossible.

He was tempted to sprint after the taxi before it gathered speed, drag Janie out and offer her, on his knees, the complete shambles he'd made of his life.

Anything would be better, he thought wretchedly, then seeing her drive off, hurt and hating him.

And what had possessed him just now—coming on to her like some macho ape? There'd been something about her pale, scornful face that had flicked him on the raw, but that was no excuse. Had he really thought such pitiful 'Me Tarzan, you Jane' tactics would have her melting in his arms?

If so, he knew differently now.

As he watched the taxi round the corner and disappear, he felt the world turn cold. It was as if he'd been suddenly washed up—abandoned on the edge of some wilderness—without food, shelter or hope.

And useless to tell himself that maybe it was for the best, he thought, as he walked slowly back indoors.

That it was hardly the optimum time to be cementing a new relationship when he was likely to find himself jobless at any moment.

The fact that he'd done the correct thing for the right motives was no consolation at all in this new hell of loneliness he'd created for himself.

His thoughts were as bleak as his face as he rode up in the lift. The call he'd just taken had been from Cilla Godwin's secretary, requiring him to present himself in the editor's office tomorrow.

The head of Features had been enthusiastic over the 'Lonely in London' series, but he wasn't expecting any compliments from Cilla. She'd been badgering him for days to have the Janie Craig piece completed and on her desk, and he didn't know what to tell her, what further excuse he could possibly formulate for withholding it.

Certainly not the truth, he thought cynically. That anything he wrote about his meetings with Janie would be tantamount to forcing them both to strip naked in public.

So far, he'd managed to finish one piece about her. He'd written far into the night, driven by some inner compulsion he hardly understood. But when he'd looked at what he'd done the next morning, he'd found himself reading a declaration of love.

That was the moment that had brought him to his senses. That had made him realise what he really felt for her.

And that was why watching her drive away had been like dying inside. Her white strained face would haunt him, he thought, until the end of his days.

Yet now, somehow, he had to drag his thoughts away from her to the problem of Cilla.

He swore softly under his breath. He'd maintained a deliberately low profile since the night she'd come to the flat, but he knew his failure to respond to her overtures would never be forgiven or forgotten. She was, he was convinced, simply awaiting an opportunity to destroy him. And, if it was inevitable, perhaps he should just lie back and let it happen, he thought wearily.

But the fighting spirit which had carried him safely through wars, riots and revolutions was reluctant to concede her so easy a victory.

He went into the bedroom and stood for a moment, looking down at the crumpled bed. He sank down on its edge and picked up the pillow Ros had used, holding it to his face, inhaling the faint fragrance of her skin which still clung there evocatively.

Waking with her in his arms had made so much clear to him. Had made him see exactly what he wanted from life. What he still had to figure was how to achieve it.

'The engagement's off,' Janie announced, marching into the kitchen. 'Ros—did you hear me?' she added sharply to the motionless figure, sitting staring into space at the kitchen table. 'What's the matter with you? Have you gone into a trance?'

Ros looked at her, startled eyes dazed as she struggled for comprehension. 'You've finished with Martin? I—I'm sorry.'

'Don't be. He's being such a pain.' Janie filled the kettle and set it down on the work surface with a thump. 'He won't budge over the wedding.' She snorted. 'I'm glad I realised how completely he's under his parents' control before it was too late.' She paused. 'Do you want some coffee? That stuff in front of you looks stone-cold.'

'It is.' Ros surrendered the mug, and watched her stepsister rinse it out.

'What's wrong?' Janie asked. 'Problems with the book? Publishers giving you the thumbs-down?'

'No,' Ros said. 'It's nothing to do with that.'

'Then what?'

Ros bit her lip. 'Just a few—personal things I need to think through.'

'Oh, God.' Jane turned an apprehensive look on her. 'You're not missing Colin?'

Colin, Ros thought. Colin belonged to another life, another age, another universe. To her shame, she hadn't even given him a thought.

'No,' she said. 'But I'm rather ducking the thought of telling him it's over.'

'Let me,' Janie offered callously. 'It'll be a pleasure.'

In spite of her unhappiness, Ros felt her lips curve in a reluctant smile. 'I thought you'd have had more sympathy—having just been through the same thing yourself.'

'Well, in my case it may not be permanent,' Janie admitted. 'I'm going to let Martin stew for a day or two. He'll come round.'

Ros stared at her, distress closing her throat. 'How can you treat him like that, if you love him?' she protested. 'Can't you imagine what it's like to watch the person you love—your one hope of happiness—just—walk out of your life? What it's like to think that you're not wanted any more? Don't you care that you're making him suffer?'

'Whatever's come over you?' Janie spooned coffee

granules into the mugs. 'Why are you so concerned about Martin? You hardly know him.'

Ros bit her lip. 'I suppose I was thinking of all lovers, and how cruel we can be to each other,' she said, after a pause.

'My word,' Janie said acidly. 'Ditching Colin has had a profound effect. Do you want your coffee black or white?'

There was no point in delaying things any longer, Ros decided. She would go and see Colin and break the news to him that evening. It wasn't a pleasant prospect, but nothing could make her feel more wretched than she already did.

Besides, Janie was going out to a club with two of the girls she was working with, and Ros wasn't looking forward to spending the evening with only her thoughts for company.

Once it's over with, I can draw a line under everything that's happened, she thought, steeling herself against the inevitable shaft of pain. Consign it all to the past and—go on. Somehow.

But go on where? And do what? She had a new life to build—maybe not only her own—and the thought made her feel restless.

Perhaps it was time she made a completely fresh start. She could write anywhere, after all. So she didn't have to stay in London, have to fight her memories every day...

She looked around her in a kind of remote wonder.

My God, she thought. I'm actually contemplating leaving this house. My prized possession. My sanctuary. This cannot be real.

If I sell, I'll be betraying Venetia. Rejecting her legacy.

She wandered out into the garden. It wasn't raining any longer, and a watery sun had struggled through the clouds.

Ros took a quick breath, absorbing the sharp scent of damp earth, And, as if a switch had clicked in her brain, saw Venetia Blake, her old gardening hat crammed on her head, secateurs in hand, moving along the path in front of her, scanning the raised bed for dead flowers.

'Of course, I love it here.' Across the years her voice reached Ros again, bringing a new clarity. 'But a house is only a place. It's the people who live in it that matter—who make it a home. Never forget that, darling.' Her smile was sudden and deeply tender. 'And this house has never meant the same to me since your grandfather died, bless him. He made it special.' She sighed. 'I should have moved, but I'm just too old and too lazy.'

And then, just as suddenly, Ros found herself alone with the chill of the evening breeze. Found, too, she was remembering the wording of her grandmother's will.

'My house…and its contents', she thought, her throat tightening, 'in the hope that she will use them properly'.

And for the first time she realised that Venetia Blake had only ever meant her to use Gilshaw Street as a staging post. And that, when the time was right, she'd expected her to move on.

In spite of her inner misery, Ros felt as if one weight, at least, had been lifted from her shoulders.

And now it was time to remove another, she thought as she went back indoors.

But she'd better let Colin know she was coming, she conceded, and reached for the phone.

It rang a couple of times and then she heard a woman's voice answer. For a second she thought it must be Mrs Hayton, and then she realised it sounded much too young.

She said, 'May I speak to Colin Hayton, please? It's Ros—Rosamund Craig.'

There was a pause, then the voice said, 'Just a minute.'

Ros waited, and was eventually assailed by another voice, which this time really did belong to Colin's mother.

'Good evening, Rosamund. This is quite a surprise.' It was an edged remark. 'Is there something you wanted?'

'Well—yes.' Ros swallowed. 'I was hoping to come over this evening to see Colin—if it's convenient, of course.'

'I fear not,' Mrs Hayton said majestically. 'We have guests.'

The mystery voice, thought Ros. And an honoured guest if she's allowed to pick up the phone. She said, 'Then when could I come?'

'I think it might be better for Colin to contact you,' Mrs Hayton decreed. 'I know he's been planning to do so.'

'I see,' Ros said slowly. 'How—how is his ankle?'

'It's responding very well to treatment.' Mrs Hayton paused. 'Fortunately he does have a few supportive people in his life,' she added with emphasis.

The only silver lining to all these clouds was that

Mrs Hayton was not going to be her mother-in-law, Ros thought, teeth gritted.

She said quietly, 'I need to talk to him urgently, Mrs Hayton. Please give him that message.'

There was a sniff and a clunk as the older woman disconnected.

Her day was not improving, Ros thought grimly, as she replaced her own receiver. And somehow she had to get through the evening.

I'll apply the usual palliatives, she decided, her mouth twisting as she flicked through her phone index. Some mindless violence from the video service, and a Chinese takeaway.

She had some sleeping pills somewhere. She'd take one to ensure she got a night's rest, then she'd be ready to face tomorrow, and all the decisions she had to make. All the heartbreak she had, somehow, to heal.

Nobody said it would be easy, she thought. But I'll survive.

Unbidden, unwanted, the image of Sam forced its way into her mind. She saw the glow in his turquoise eyes, the slant of his smile, and felt her whole body recoil in anguish.

Because she didn't want merely to survive. She wanted to live every moment of her life to the full. And without Sam that was impossible. Because without him she was only half a person.

She wrapped her arms round her body and began to rock slowly, as the first tears scalded her face.

Sam, she whispered silently, desolately. Sam—what have you done to me? To us?

And why do I still have to love you so much?

*   *   *

'Sam. Good of you to spare me the time.' Cilla Godwin's smile held an unpromising glitter as she waved him to a chair.

'I wasn't aware I had a choice,' Sam returned coldly. 'And I won't sit, thanks. I prefer to receive bad news standing.'

'Oh, but all the news is good. As I'm sure he's told you, Phil's delighted with your work on the series—so far, that is. There is still one piece missing, but I'm sure you're dealing with that.'

There was something badly wrong here, Sam realised, all his hackles rising. But what?

'I feel we have to make optimum use of your investigative talents,' she went on. 'And I have a few ideas which I'll discuss with you in due time.

'But first we have to decide how to promote this lonely hearts series—particularly as you've just won this award. A big publicity campaign, I think. National advertising. Billboards and television. "Award-winning Sam Hunter goes undercover—and how". Something on those lines. Splashes in the *Echo*, with photographs, naturally.'

Her laugh was like ice cubes falling into an empty tumbler—only not as pleasant.

'I'm going to make you famous, Sam. Or, from another viewpoint, infamous,' she added musingly.

'No,' Sam said, his voice ominously even. 'You can't do that. Phil guaranteed to print the stuff under another name, to protect the interviewees. I've been careful not to identify them too closely, so the chances are they won't recognise themselves even if they read the *Echo*.

'But if you do this, it blows the whole thing out of the water.' He leaned forward across the wide desk, his eyes boring into hers. 'God, Cilla, they're fragile people. If they realise they've been set up, it could do real damage.'

'You're all heart. But the decision's mine. Not Phil's. And certainly not yours.' She picked up a pen from her desk and began to play with it, her fingers moving suggestively over the barrel. 'And you don't have any power to influence things.' Her voice was soft, almost sweet. 'Which was your decision. If you remember.'

'Oh, I remember,' Sam said between his teeth. 'Women aren't immune from accusations of sexual harassment. Maybe you should remember that.'

She shrugged. 'It would be your word against mine. A pathetic attempt at revenge by a disappointed man. Or that's how the tribunal would see it. I'd make quite sure of that.' She smiled again. 'I'm certain that's not the image you want. Besides, your own behaviour doesn't bear close scrutiny,' she added, almost casually. 'We could be looking at breach of contract here, instant dismissal with no comeback.'

'What are you talking about?' Sam felt a sudden chill.

She opened a drawer, produced a folder, and pushed it towards him.

'You've been taking far too long over this Janie Craig interview, and I started wondering why. So I designated someone to keep an eye on you, and yesterday it paid off.'

The photograph spilled out towards him. They were good, some part of him acknowledged. A man and a girl locked together in passion and pain on a London street, their mouths devouring each other. The girl walking away, her eyes like black holes in her strained, tense face. The man watching her go with hunger and regret.

His heart was suddenly like a stone in his chest. He thought, Oh, darling...

'And don't tell me that's not Janie Craig, Sam.' Her glance stabbed him malevolently. 'Because we know that it is. And you had orders not to get personally involved. To look, and talk, but not to touch. I'd say this went much further than touching—wouldn't you? A serious breach of professional conduct,' she added jeeringly. 'Meriting sacking without notice and loss of all financial benefits.'

She paused. 'I'd also make sure you never worked on another national paper. So, if you want to keep your job, and the lifestyle that comes with it, stay in line and do what I tell you. I shall look forward to reading about your exploits with your little beautician. Try not to make them too pornographic.'

She reached for some papers. 'You can go now,' she added casually.

'One more thing.' Sam stood his ground, his gaze and voice level. 'When does this advertising campaign begin?'

'Next week, so that it can peak at the awards ceremony. The highpoint of your career, Sam.' She flicked him with a malicious glance. 'Make the most of it, darling. Things will never be this good again.'

'On the contrary.' Sam walked to the door, and paused. The turquoise eyes were calm, even a little pitying as he looked back at her. His smile was relaxed, and without anger. 'You've made me see that they can only get better.'

*   *   *

Janie, Sam thought, as he ran down to the car park. He had to see her, tell her the truth about his real identity before she saw it plastered all over the hoardings.

He'd intended to do it anyway, but now it was a question of much sooner rather than later.

As he drew up in Gilshaw Street, a dark woman with a sunny smile was outside, giving the brass a vigorous polishing.

'Hello, you must be Manuela.' He gave her a coaxing grin. 'Is Janie at home?'

She shook her head regretfully. 'She is at work. You see her there.'

Sam groaned. 'Except I don't know which store she's at. Have you any idea?'

She looked him up and down with an approving twinkle. 'She has list of jobs in kitchen. I find out for you.'

She was back in no time, with a slip of paper bearing the name of a major West End store. 'She is here. The company name is Beauty Queen.'

'I'll find her.' Sam ran down the steps to the car. 'Manuela, you're a star,' he tossed back over his shoulder.

Manuela went back to her polishing with a sigh. Why were the interesting men attracted only to the little Juanita? she wondered. She was pretty, *sí*, but the señorita Rosa was a truly lovely girl—so warm—so kind. When would it be her turn?

But, she thought, shrugging, who would she meet, shut away as she was at the top of the house, with a computer, writing another book?

She sighed again, and forgot the whole incident.

The ground floor of the store was crowded with shoppers, but there was a large banner advertising the

Beauty Queen promotion and Sam fought his way towards it.

He hadn't worked out how he was going to persuade her to listen to him. She might walk away. She might even slap his face. But he'd deal with it all when it happened.

I just want to see her, he thought, feeling his heart muscles clench.

It would be such a relief to tell her everything at last, with no more pretence and no more secrets.

I thought I had no choice, he told himself. But I was wrong, and I'll admit it on my knees if I have to.

However badly she reacted, he would win her round somehow. Because he needed her as he needed air to breathe.

The fact that she was nowhere to be seen was a total anticlimax.

Perhaps Manuela had got the whole thing wrong, Sam thought with an inward groan.

'May I help you?' A pretty blonde in a strawberry-pink suit smiled at him.

He said, 'Actually, I'm looking for someone—a demonstrator here. Her name's Janie Craig. Do you know her?'

The smile became slightly rigid. 'Is this a joke?'

'No,' he said swiftly. 'No, it's absolutely serious, and pretty urgent. I need to find her now. My name's Sam—Sam Alexander.'

There was an electric silence. The girl's pink mouth formed an 'O' of total astonishment. She took a step backwards, her eyes looking him up and down in frank appraisal. Then she laughed.

'Hi, there,' she said. 'I'm Janie Craig. And you, of course, must be "Lonely in London". So we get to meet after all.'

CHAPTER ELEVEN

IT HADN'T been a productive morning, Ros acknowledged wearily as she came out of her office and started downstairs. But it was hard to give full weight to her heroine's romantic problems when her own were tearing her apart.

She'd have a break, something to eat, even though she wasn't hungry, then try again.

'You are so pale today.' Manuela gave her a concerned look as she entered the kitchen. 'You are ill?'

Sick at heart, Ros thought. If that counts.

She said, 'I'm fine, Manuela. I just didn't sleep very well last night.'

'You should take better care of yourself. Be like Miss Juanita and not worry.'

'Oh, Janie has her problems too,' Ros said wryly. 'She's quarrelled with her boyfriend.'

'No more.' Manuela pursed her lips. 'He came to look for her—to make up—but he didn't know where she was working, so I told him.'

'Martin came here?' Ros's brows lifted. 'You should have let me know,' she commented drily. 'I could have given him some sisterly advice.'

'You were working. He was in big hurry.' Manuela accepted her money, and went off cheerfully.

It looked as if Martin was caving in over the wedding, Ros thought frowningly, as she made herself a sandwich, and she wasn't sure that was a good thing. It would be far healthier for Janie to be thwarted occasionally, and made to see that other people had valid points of view.

She was just about to take a bite of sandwich when the phone rang.

A man's voice said, 'Is that Rosamund Craig?'

She said, 'Speaking,' and stopped dead, her eyes widening as she suddenly recognised her caller's voice. She said, faltering slightly, 'Sam—it's you...'

And heard the phone go down, cutting her off with a kind of awful finality.

When her mind cleared, she found she was kneeling on the floor, whispering, 'Oh, God,' over and over again.

He's found out, she thought desperately. He knows who I really am—and that I've been lying to him all this time. Pretending to be Janie. But how?

Shakily, she remembered Manuela's beaming account of their morning visitor. The man she'd assumed was Martin—and sent off to find the real Janie...

That had to be the answer.

I should have told him myself, she berated herself. Confessed that first night. Because after that it never seemed to be the right time. And now it's too late.

It's all—too late.

She threw away the uneaten sandwich, and went upstairs to her room. Her mouth curled with distaste as she surveyed the tearstained, bedraggled figure in her mirror.

She couldn't face the world looking like this. And she'd no doubt she'd have to face it—principally in the shape of Janie, who'd be erupting through the front door, demanding an explanation, in just a couple of hours.

But I've no explanation to offer, she thought wretchedly. Not one that makes sense, anyway. I can hardly say I was just following her advice—going out to meet life head-on.

Yet how can I tell her the truth? That I met a stranger, and fell in love with him almost before I knew it. That's ridiculous too. Because I don't do things like that. Or the person I used to be never did. The girl I am now is capable of anything. She could even be expecting a baby by a man who doesn't want to know.

And she's brought it all—*all* on herself.

There was a taste of tears in her throat, and she swallowed them back. There was no point in crying any more. Now she had to pull herself together, and sort out what was left of her life.

She'd have a bath, she thought, and shampoo her hair. If she looked better, she might feel marginally better too.

She'd just finished drying her hair when she heard the doorbell. The dryer slipped from her hand and fell to the carpet unheeded.

She whispered, 'Sam,' and flew downstairs, tightening the sash on her towelling robe as she went. As she reached the hall, the bell sounded again.

He was certainly impatient, Ros thought as she fumbled with the chain, fingers made clumsy by haste. He was undoubtedly very angry. But at least he was here, and prepared to talk. So there was hope. Of a kind. Wasn't there?

She flung open the door and stood for moment, feeling her jaw drop with surprise and disappointment.

'So you are at home,' said Colin, his tone cool.

'You said you wanted to see me. Aren't you going to ask me in?'

She said, dry-mouthed, 'Yes—yes, of course,' and stood aside as he limped into the hall, leaning on a walking stick.

'But there was no need for you to come all this way,' she said, following him into the sitting room. 'Put yourself to all this trouble. I was prepared to go to you. I said so to your mother.'

'We decided it would be better this way,' he said. 'Less awkward. And my ankle's much improved. I've been having brilliant physiotherapy.'

'Oh,' she said. 'Well—that's good.'

He nodded. 'It's time we met up, Ros. We haven't seen each other for quite some time. And there are certain things—things about the future—that we need to discuss.'

She swallowed. 'Colin—I...'

'Hear me out, please.' He lifted a hand. 'There's no easy way to say this to you—not after all the time we've been together, the plans we've made. But the fact is I—I've met someone else. And we're going to be married.'

For a moment she stared at him incredulously, then she threw back her head and started to laugh uncontrollably.

'Oh, God,' Colin muttered. 'You're hysterical. I was afraid of this. I wanted to break it to you more gently, but Mother said there was no point in beating about the bush, and Valerie agreed with her.'

'No.' Ros wiped her streaming eyes. 'No, I'm fine, I promise you. Look—totally straight face. Totally normal human being.' She took a deep breath. 'I gather Valerie's your new fiancée. How on earth did you meet her when you couldn't walk?'

'She's the physiotherapist,' he said eagerly. 'The one who brought me home after I did the initial damage. She started driving down to give me treatment each day.' He looked slightly shamefaced. 'And then she stopped driving back.' He paused. 'Ros, I'm so sorry. I feel such a heel…'

'No,' she said gently. 'No, you mustn't. It wasn't working for us—not any more. And we both sensed it. But you did something about it. And I'm happy for you.'

'Really? You mean it?'

I bet his mother told him I'd be clinging to his knees, begging him not to go, thought Ros.

She said, 'Absolutely. It's terrific news.'

On his way to the door, something occurred to him. 'Is that what you wanted to say to me?'

'More or less,' she agreed levelly.

'Oh,' he said. 'That's all right, then.' He hesitated. 'Valerie drove me over, and she's parked a few doors away. Would—would you like to meet her?'

'I'm hardly dressed for guests,' she pointed out, grimacing at the old robe. 'Another time, perhaps.'

'Yes,' he said. 'Another time.'

They smiled at each other with slight awkwardness, both knowing that there would be no other time.

On the doorstep, he deposited a clumsy peck on her cheek, then hobbled gingerly down the steps. Ros breathed a silent sigh of relief when he reached the bottom in safety, knowing that if he'd fallen his mother would have sworn she'd pushed him.

She was just about to turn away and shut the door

when an odd prickle of awareness alerted her to the
fact that she was being watched in turn.

The unknown Valerie, she wondered, riding shotgun
on her man?

She glanced casually up the street and saw Sam,
leaning against his car and staring at her.

She gripped the metal rail, feeling it bite into her
hand, waiting as he walked slowly towards her and up
the steps.

'Who was that?' His voice was terse.

'Colin,' she said. 'The man I used to see.'

His mouth twisted bitterly. 'You didn't waste any
time.'

'No,' she said. 'It's not what you think...'

'But then what is?' His smile grazed her. The look
in his eyes made her shiver. 'Well—are you going to
ask me in, my Fair Rosamund—my Rose of the
World—or are we going to stay here and give the
locals another field-day?'

She led the way into the sitting room. 'You saw
Janie.' It was a statement not a question.

'Yes,' he said. 'She was most informative about her
sister the bestselling novelist, who was also fortunate
enough to be left a house worth at least four hundred
grand.' He whistled. '*Very* impressive. So what were
you doing with me, darling? Slumming? Did you
fancy a bit of rough?'

She winced, scared by the anger in his voice.
'Sam—don't. It wasn't like that.'

'No,' he said. 'I forgot. You told me. It was duty.
Sometimes above and beyond the call—' his eyes
stripped the robe away '—but I'm not complaining.'

'Say what you want,' she said quietly. 'I suppose I
deserve it.'

'I knew from the start there was something wrong,' he said. 'Something that didn't quite ring true. That was what intrigued me. But I never guessed the extent of your little charade. Never realised that the girl I'd fallen in love with didn't exist. That you were simply playing a game that went a little too far.'

'You fell in love with me?' Her voice shook. 'That's the first time you've said that.'

'Well, don't let it bother you.' His tone was scornful. 'I shan't let it trouble me.'

'And it wasn't a game. You must believe me.'

'Now you're asking the impossible. So, what was it, then, my sweet? A plot for you latest novel?'

She remembered her hero with the turquoise eyes, and betraying colour warmed her face.

He noticed, of course. 'My God,' he said slowly. 'I was right. You were using me as copy. What a joke. And what an amazing coincidence.'

'I don't know what you mean.'

'I meant the ad in the *Clarion* was a put-up job—placed there by the Features department of the *Daily Echo*.' He watched her absorb that and nodded grimly. 'I was assigned to investigate the lonely hearts scene—from the inside. Meet Sam Alexander Hunter, ace reporter.' He sketched a mocking bow.

'So,' he went on, 'while you were using me, I was using you too. Both biters well and truly bitten. There's a certain poignant justice in the situation—don't you think?'

She said again, 'Sam,' her voice a whisper.

'I felt so guilty about you,' he continued, as if he hadn't heard her. 'I couldn't write a word of the piece about you. And I've been tearing myself to pieces over deceiving you. Because you were wonderful—my perfect, unique girl.' He laughed harshly. 'And now I find I've been blaming myself for nothing. Because you're no better than I am.'

Ros flung back her head. 'I'm sorry if I didn't fit your pedestal. But I didn't ask to be measured for it. I never meant any of this to happen. Janie was going to stand you up, and I decided to take her place. For one evening, that was all. Because I didn't want you to be disappointed. But once it had started there seemed no way back.'

'There's always a way back,' he said. 'I came to find you today to warn you that the *Echo* are launching a major campaign to publicise the series and blowing my cover in the process. I was going to tell you everything, and ask you to forgive me. To give me another chance. How many kinds of fool does that make me?' he asked savagely.

'Can't we—forgive each other?' She was trembling.

'There's no need,' he said. 'We're back at square one. I've now met Janie, and she tells me she's still "Looking for Love". It's all worked out neatly.'

Her mouth felt numb. 'You—and Janie?'

'You have some objection?' He paused. 'She's a little—stunned by everything that's happened, so she's decided to stay away for a few days. I'm sure you understand. If you'll put some things in a bag for her, I'll see she gets them.'

She lifted her chin. 'Of course. Will she—be staying with you?'

He smiled. 'I don't think that's any of your business. Do you?'

She had to behave with dignity, she told herself as she packed Janie's weekend case with toiletries, underwear and a change of clothes. Because dignity seemed all she had left.

She felt as if she'd been wounded and left to die on some battlefield. Her world was reeling. She was sick, and frightened, and in terrible pain.

And presently she was going to have to watch Sam walk out of her life for ever—and go to Janie.

She thought, I can't bear it. But I must—somehow.

He was waiting in the hall. She handed him the case.

'I hope I haven't forgotten anything.'

'I can get her anything else she wants.'

She said huskily, 'You do realise she's engaged?'

'I gather it's in abeyance at the moment.' He shrugged.

'And that makes it all right?'

'It's a bit late to occupy the moral high ground, Ros,' he said harshly. 'So just leave it out.'

He walked to the door. 'It's been an instructive interlude, for both of us. I'm not sure I can wish you well, but I hope your book sells as many copies as my newspaper. Because that's what it's all about in the end. And we both have our lives to pay for.'

'Will you go, please?' Her voice shook.

'One last thing,' he said. He put the case down and walked back to her. She tried to step away, but his hands descended on her shoulders, anchoring her. His voice slowed to a drawl. 'Do satisfy my curiosity, darling. Are you wearing anything under that robe?' He reached down and untied the sash, then drew the edges apart. 'No, I thought not. No wonder the boyfriend needed a walking stick.'

She said unevenly, 'You bastard.'

'I try.' His hand stroked the length of her body, and

she had to grit her teeth to avoid crying her need, her yearning aloud. But she wouldn't give him that satisfaction.

He bent, and she felt his mouth fasten fiercely on to her breast.

As he raised his head, the crooked smile he sent her pierced her heart.

'My brand,' he said softly, touching the small red mark with his fingertip. 'But don't worry, my love. It will fade. Everything does—in time. Or so they tell me. We'll just have to wait and see.'

She stood. Eyes closed, so that she did not have to see any more. Hands pressed over her ears, so that she would not hear the door closing or his car drive away.

But she could not silence the clamour of her flesh, or the black, empty loneliness which had invaded her soul.

She thought, He's gone. And now I have nothing left. Nothing.

And she began to cry like a child raging against a world it does not understand.

CHAPTER TWELVE

'BUT of course you're going to the award ceremony,' Vivien said severely. 'I accepted on your behalf.'

Ros sighed. 'I know. But that was then. This is now. And I don't feel like dressing up and going out. Especially if people are going to look at me and I have to make a speech.'

'Then that's exactly the time you should dress up and go out,' said Vivien. 'It will do you good. You've been looking washed out for weeks.' She paused, giving Ros a shrewd look. 'You are all right? I mean, there's nothing the matter—nothing that you should see a doctor about?'

'No.' A small, sad pain twisted inside her. 'There's—nothing wrong.' *Not even that. Not even Sam's baby.*

'Then treat yourself to some blusher,' said Vivien briskly. 'And you don't have to make a speech. You just thank them nicely for the rose bowl. It's not the Oscars,' she added. 'You don't have to mention everyone you've ever known. Oh, and thank them for the cheque as well. Although heaven knows you don't need the money after what you've been offered for your house.' She paused. 'Have you decided where you're going to live yet?'

'No. I might wander around for a while. See all the parts of Britain I've never visited before I decide.'

'But after you've finished your book, I hope?' There was a touch of anxiety in her editor's voice.

'Yes.' Ros tried a reassuring smile. 'The Cuthberts don't want to move in immediately, so I'll have plenty of time to do that. And then I'll probably rent somewhere while I write the next book.'

'Any idea what it's going to be about?'

Ros shook her head. 'Not yet.'

She usually had several ideas jockeying for position, but not this time. She couldn't think that far ahead. She was managing—just—to live one day at a time.

She could write the current book because it seemed to bring her closer to Sam. Because she could fabricate the happy ending for her heroine that she'd been denied. And that, she found, was strangely comforting.

There wasn't a great deal else to be happy about.

Janie had eventually returned, but had been unusually reticent, volunteering no information about where she'd been or what she'd been doing.

But then, Ros thought unhappily, maybe she would rather not know at that...

On the first evening she'd said, 'Janie—you must be wondering...'

'I did at first.' Janie shrugged. 'But not any more. And you don't need to explain. It happened, and it's all finished, anyway, so you don't have to beat yourself with it.'

Ros bit her lip. 'Perhaps I need to.'

'No.' Janie shook her head. 'Everyone makes a complete idiot of themselves somewhere along the line. It just took you longer than most people, but you got there in the end. And that's all there is to it. *Finito.*'

It seemed that her relationship with Martin was equally *finito*. When Ros ventured to ask if they were still seeing each other, she got a flat, 'No.'

'I'm sorry,' Ros said quietly.

'Don't be. I realise now I was never really in love with him. I was just hung up on the marriage and babies scene. But none of that has to be a priority. There are other things in life.'

And she relapsed into silence, leaving Ros to draw her own unhappy conclusions.

It was the nearest to a confidence that they approached, because things were not the same between them. Every time Janie left the house, Ros found herself wondering if she was going to see Sam, but dared not ask. And, which was worse, Janie seemed to be silently challenging her to do so. When the phone rang Ros avoided answering it, using the machine as a shield.

Therefore it was almost a relief when Janie abruptly announced that she and Pam had booked a last-minute holiday in Minorca and were flying out the following week.

By the time she returned their parents would be back from their trip, and that would ease the pressure too, or so Ros hoped.

What she couldn't avoid was seeing Sam's picture plastered over hoardings and bus shelters, with banner headlines promising lurid revelations about the singles scene.

She could not, she knew, hope to escape unscathed. But wondering how much he was going to reveal about their relationship was driving her slowly mad.

At last, despising herself, she took a taxi round to his flat. But although she rang the bell and knocked until her knuckles felt bruised, there was no answer.

'Did you want Mr Hunter?' An elderly woman

emerged from the opposite flat. 'I'm afraid you won't find him. He's gone away and the flat's to let.'

'Oh,' Ros said numbly. 'I—I didn't know.'

The other nodded. 'It was a shock for me too. He was always so kind. An ideal neighbour.' She sighed. 'Ah, well. Nothing lasts for ever.' She smiled at Ros, and turned away.

No, Ros thought. Nothing lasts.

On her way back to Chelsea she called in at an estate agents and put her house on the market. And forty-eight hours later it was sold.

She bought a new dress for the awards ceremony, simple and stylish in black silk, cut on the bias, with a skirt that fluttered around her knees as she walked. The sleeveless bodice was held up by thin straps and the neckline dipped deeply towards her breasts. The matching cape was lined in silver.

As she walked into the Palais Royal on Park Lane, she wondered vaguely who her fellow winners were. Vivien, she thought, had mentioned that the journalism award had gone to someone who'd covered the Mzruban civil war and just escaped with his life. But that was as much as she knew.

The first thing she saw in the foyer were two giant blown-up photographs of herself and Sam side by side. The shock of it stopped her in her tracks.

What was this? she asked herself frantically. Was someone playing some monstrous joke?

Vivien came through the groups of chattering people. 'What is it?' she demanded. 'You look as if you've seen a ghost.'

'That's how I feel.' Ros pointed at Sam's photograph. 'What's that doing here?'

'He's the journalist I told you about,' Vivien said patiently. 'The extremely un-civil war. Remember?'

Ros swallowed. 'He's not actually here tonight, is he?'

'I've no idea,' Vivien retorted. 'He's not my responsibility, thank God. Getting you up to the mark was problem enough.' She paused. 'Anyway, what's wrong with Sam Hunter? Very sexy guy, they tell me, and unattached, although there have been rumours recently that he's seeing someone.'

Ros bit her lip. 'Actually,' she said, 'I think I've mistaken him for someone else.'

Before the awards dinner there were drinks for the winners in a private room, hosted by *Life Today* magazine.

Ros was handed a glass of champagne, and chatted to the magazine's editor, Henry Garland, a genial, bearded man with a booming laugh. Ros tried to smile appreciatively at his jokes, and respond to his remarks, but her concentration was shot to pieces. She'd scanned the room as she entered, but, to her relief, there was no sign of Sam. Now she was sneaking constant glances at the door, expecting it to open and admit him at any moment.

She was thankful when Henry Garland moved on to greet someone else.

'That's Cilla Godwin over there,' Vivien hissed in her ear. 'She's the new editor of the *Echo*. I wonder what she's done with her golden boy.'

Ros gave a casual glance in the direction indicated and encountered a look of such dislike that she almost took a step backwards.

'I wonder what she's done with common civility,'

she muttered back. 'And isn't she a little old for that dress?'

Vivien patted her approvingly. 'Well done. You're coming back to life. Funnily enough, she was asking about you earlier.'

Ros stiffened. 'She was?'

'Yes, she cornered me in the powder room and said wasn't your real name Janie, and hadn't you once worked as a make-up girl? I said she was confusing you with your stepsister, and I thought she was going to have a heart attack. I've never seen anyone so angry.'

'How—very odd,' Ros said faintly. 'I hope she doesn't—corner me.'

'Don't worry,' said Vivien. 'Our table's at the opposite end of the room from the *Echo*. Oh, good, they're calling us in to dinner. And mind you eat properly and put back some of the weight you've lost,' she added.

'Yes, Mother,' said Ros, her mouth curving reluctantly in her first real smile of the evening.

She dutifully swallowed her portion of the vegetable terrine, and the chicken in wine sauce that followed. She even managed some of the chocolate roulade, but was thankful when coffee was served.

The *Echo*'s table might be at the other end of the room, but the empty chair next to Cilla Godwin's was clearly visible, even when she didn't crane her neck.

She glanced restively at her watch, calculating how long it would take to receive her award, make polite noises, and escape.

She waited while the non-fiction award was made to a travel writer, and the prize for children's writing was also handed over. Then it was her turn.

She stood, holding the rose bowl and the cheque, while Henry Garland congratulated her on the popularity of her novels and their worldwide sales success. As he finished, she moved to the microphone and began her few planned words of appreciation. She was aware of a stir in the audience, and glanced up instinctively.

Sam had appeared in the doorway at the back of the room. He was lounging against a doorpost, seemingly relaxed, but as their eyes met Ros felt as if she'd encountered an electrical urge.

The words died on her lips. She tried to recapture her thread, failed, and said, 'Thank you all so much,' in a small, nervous voice, and dashed off the stage.

'Now you know why I don't do public appearances,' she told Vivien as she slid into her chair.

'They're applauding, not throwing things. You did fine.' Vivien was warmly consoling. 'Shy is this year's flavour. Unlike the "in your face—I'll break your legs" attitude of Ms Godwin.' She nudged Ros. 'I see her foreign ace has finally arrived.'

'Yes,' Ros said, dry-mouthed. She paused. 'Would anyone notice if I slipped away?'

'The whole room, I should think.' Vivien was firm. 'It won't take much longer. There's television writing next, and then it's Sam Hunter—who, may I say, is much dishier than his photograph.'

She had a point, Ros admitted. Sam was wearing dinner jacket and black tie, like all the other men present, but on his tall figure the formal dress had an added distinction. His dark hair had grown back to its normal length, too, and looked attractively tousled.

As if, she thought, he'd just got out of bed...

She sat staring at her cooling coffee as he mounted

the platform to receive his award, amid enthusiastic applause.

When the room quietened, he began to speak, his voice cool and slightly sardonic.

'I'm grateful to *Life Today* for giving me this award,' he said. 'Because it will always remind me that I was once a half-decent writer. Something I almost lost sight of.

'I was proud of my civil war coverage. But I'm certainly not proud of my most recent assignment, which many of you will have seen advertised.

'I'd like to take this opportunity to apologise to all the decent women who were fooled into giving me their time and attention. I found the whole episode shameful, but there has been an up-side. It helped clarify once and for all what I want from life, and how I want to live it. And I know this isn't the *Echo*, in spite of all the financial advantages. They mattered once, but not any more. They can chain someone else to their treadmill. I prefer my freedom.

'The "Lonely in London" feature also, and most unexpectedly, introduced me to the woman I hope to marry. So who says personal columns don't work?'

There was a concerted gasp, and then a ripple of applause. At the *Echo* table, Cilla Godwin appeared to have turned to granite.

'This award is particularly precious because it's the last one I'll ever get,' he went on. 'I'm quitting national journalism altogether, to join a weekly paper in the Yorkshire Dales. Nominally, I'm editor, but I suspect I shall also be making the coffee and accepting small ads. It's that kind of set-up, and I can hardly wait. At the moment there's no personal column, but that's my first planned change.'

He held up the rose bowl. 'Roses are my favourite flower—particularly Rosa Mundi—the Rose of the World. I look forward to seeing this filled with them.

'And the cheque will pay the deposit on a house I've seen—if my bride-to-be approves. So—a heartfelt thank-you to you all.'

The whole room was on its feet applauding as he left the platform, apart from those at the *Echo* table, who stayed in their seats, transfixed by a look from Godzilla.

Ros said in an undertone, 'I must go.' She sped out into the reception area, where staff were doing some desultory clearing up, and pressed the bell for the lift, fretting as she waited for it to descend from the top floor.

A hand closed on her shoulder, and Sam said softly, 'Nice try, darling. Now we're going to talk.'

He steered her across to the room where the drinks party had been held.

'Excuse me, sir, that's a private room,' called a voice.

'Excellent,' Sam said affably, and closed the door behind them, fastening the small brass bolt as he did so. 'And that's real privacy.'

Her heart was beating so hard she felt suffocated. She confronted him, head high. 'Will you let me go, please?'

'Yes,' he said. 'Eventually. If that's what you really want. But first you're going to listen.'

'Say what you want.' Ros said curtly. She sat down on a small gilt chair. 'What difference does it make?'

'All the difference in the world, I hope.' He shook his head. 'We're both supposed to be professional communicators, but when we're together it all goes wrong.'

'Then maybe we should cut our losses.'

'No,' he said. 'We should try again. We've made a mess of being together in the past, but when we're apart the world becomes a living hell of loneliness and cold. You're the other half of me, Ros, and I can't let you go.

'I know I've nothing much to offer. You're a high income lady, with a beautiful house, and I can't match that. The salary's a fraction of what I was earning on the *Echo*, and the house is made of grey stone, with a garden and a view. I know you'd be making a terrible sacrifice.'

His voice deepened, became passionate. 'But it's a real place to live, with real people, and it's offering me a life with some quality—some integrity. But even that won't mean anything if you're not there to share it with me.'

She said huskily, 'Why did you say none of this before?'

'Because I didn't know about the job then—just that I had to leave the *Echo*. Get out before I was destroyed. And I couldn't ask you to marry me if I was going to be out of work.

'I'm not a New Man, Ros. I want to be able to support my woman—and my children. And I want our baby to be born with my name, and my ring on your finger, however old-fashioned that is.

'And I needed my pride back—and my sense of humour—before I could come to you.'

He went down on one knee in front of her, his eyes urgently searching her face. 'Let's face it, darling. If tonight's prizes were for admirable behaviour, neither of us would qualify. But we don't have to let past mistakes poison the future.'

She looked down at her clasped hands. 'What about Janie?' she said in a low voice. 'You were—seeing her.'

'Yes,' he said. 'To collect material for my lonely hearts piece. But she was staying with her friend Pam, not me.'

'Was that her choice?'

'I don't think I gave her the option,' he said carefully. 'Your stepsister is very pretty, but she's not irresistible, and I think she found that a shock. She's clearly been riding roughshod over some poor bastard. Maybe the next man along will find her easier to deal with.'

Ros looked at him open-mouthed. 'You turned her down.'

'Of course.' His tongue was matter-of-fact. 'I belong to you, and no one else will do for me. And I shall maintain that stance until you prove to me I haven't a hope—and probably long afterwards.'

'But you let me think that you wanted her.'

'I'd just found you next door to naked with another man,' he retorted. 'I was jealous and hurting, and I wanted to hit back. I'm not proud of it.'

He took her hands in his, and she let a soft ripple of excitement tremble through her body.

She said hurriedly, 'How—how did you hear about the job?'

'From Alec Norton, who used to run the *Echo*.' His thumbs were stroking her palms. 'He's up there convalescing, and he called to say that the editor was retiring and they were looking for someone to take his place.' He smiled. 'Locally, it's regarded as a job for life. They like stability. So I went up for an interview and they offered me the job.'

'You left your flat...' Her voice died into silence as Sam lifted her hands to his lips.

'A colleague on the *Echo* is taking over the tenancy. When I've not been in Yorkshire, I've been staying at my parents' house.'

He shook his head. 'And that's been a total nightmare. Everywhere I looked there were all these memories of you, and it was driving me crazy, especially at night.

'I told myself you'd probably never want to see me again—but I had to try.' He put his cheek against her black-stockinged knee. 'Have mercy on me, Ros. Tell me that ''Lonely in London'' hasn't ruined everything for us both. At least it brought us together.'

He looked up at her, the turquoise eyes pleading. 'Is it too much to ask? Does your life in Chelsea mean too much to you?'

She slid off the chair and knelt beside him, her arms going round his neck. She said, 'I've sold my house. I was going away somewhere—anywhere—because I couldn't bear being without you. And I'd love a house in Yorkshire, with children—and a view. As long as you're there.'

For a moment he held her closely. He whispered, '''Live with me and be my love'',' then he began to kiss her, his warm, questing mouth banishing the chill of loneliness for ever. And Ros surrendered gladly, her body aglow with a happiness she had not dreamed was possible.

When she could speak, she said, 'But there isn't going to be a baby, Sam. Not yet. I know that definitely now.'

He lifted her to her feet. He said softly, 'Then let's go home and practise.' And kissed her again.

Ros removed the final page from the printer and put it neatly with the rest of the manuscript. She moved her shoulders, putting a testing hand to the small of her back.

She was glad that she'd finished the new book before the baby came, although she suspected it was going to be a closer finish than she'd realised.

Vivien, she thought happily, had better start packing her godmother's outfit.

She went over to the window and looked out. The small first-floor room she'd commandeered as a study at the back of the house overlooked the vegetable patch where Sam was digging, vigorously assisted by their golden retriever puppy.

As if he sensed her presence at the window, Sam looked up, shading his eyes, and blew her a kiss.

Ros smiled, resting her fingertips lightly against the glass, feeling her love for him open like a flower within her.

Her case was packed and waiting in the freshly decorated nursery next door. But she wouldn't tell Sam about the slight contractions she was having. Not quite yet. In case he panicked and started phoning their respective parents, and insisting she go into hospital immediately.

Because she'd rather spend her waiting time here, quietly, with him, in this home they'd made together.

In the end they'd combined their cheques from *Life Today* to provide the deposit, while, at Sam's suggestion, the money from the Chelsea house had been set aside as a trust fund for their children.

She'd go downstairs, she thought, and make some coffee, and they would sit on their verandah and drink it, and look at their view with a contentment that went too deep for words.

Sam was walking up the path towards the house, his spade on his shoulder, the dog leaping excitedly beside him.

My family, she thought, placing an exultant hand on her abdomen. My life.

Then, moving slowly, with the dignity befitting a heavily pregnant lady, Rosamund Hunter went down to join her husband.

CELEBRATE VALENTINE'S DAY WITH HARLEQUIN®'S LATEST TITLE—

Stolen Memories

Available in trade-size format, this collector's edition contains three full-length novels by *New York Times* bestselling authors Jayne Ann Krentz and Tess Gerritsen, along with national bestselling author Stella Cameron.

TEST OF TIME by Jayne Ann Krentz—

He married for the best reason.... She married for the only reason.... Did they stand a chance at making the only reason the real reason to share a lifetime?

THIEF OF HEARTS by Tess Gerritsen—

Their distrust of each other was only as strong as their desire. And Jordan began to fear that Diana was more than just a thief of hearts.

MOONTIDE by Stella Cameron—

For Andrew, Greer's return is a miracle. It had broken his heart to let her go. Now fate has brought them back together. And he won't lose her again...

Make this Valentine's Day one to remember!

Look for this exciting collector's edition on sale January 2001 at your favorite retail outlet.

HARLEQUIN®

Makes any time special ™

Visit us at www.eHarlequin.com

PHSM

#1 *New York Times* bestselling author

NORA ROBERTS

brings you more of the loyal and loving,
tempestuous and tantalizing Stanislaski family.

Coming in February 2001

The Stanislaski Sisters

Natasha and Rachel

Though raised in the Old World traditions of their
family, fiery Natasha Stanislaski and cool, classy
Rachel Stanislaski are ready for a *new* world of love....

*And also available in February 2001 from
Silhouette Special Edition, the newest book in the
heartwarming Stanislaski saga*

CONSIDERING KATE

Natasha and Spencer Kimball's daughter Kate turns her
back on old dreams and returns to her hometown, where
she finds the *man* of her dreams.

Available at your favorite retail outlet.

Where love comes alive™

He's a man of cool sophistication.
He's got pride, power and wealth.
He's a ruthless businessman, an expert lover—
and he's one hundred percent committed
to staying single.

Until now. Because suddenly he's responsible
for a BABY!

HIS BABY

An exciting miniseries from Harlequin Presents®
**He's sexy, he's successful...
and now he's facing up to fatherhood!**

On sale February 2001:
RAFAEL'S LOVE-CHILD
by Kate Walker, Harlequin Presents® #2160

On sale May 2001:
MORGAN'S SECRET SON
by Sara Wood, Harlequin Presents® #2180

And look out for more later in the year!

Available wherever Harlequin books are sold.

HARLEQUIN®
Makes any time special™

Visit us at www.eHarlequin.com   HPBABY

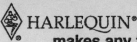